# THE BAY OF NOON

Gianni still held my arm, and still I stood there with the backs of my legs touching the cool metal frame of the bed. The cries from the sea, which throughout this time had gone unheard, were all at once raucous and urgent, as if someone had unthinkingly turned up their volume. "So thin, Jenny," Gianni repeated, to pass the time, it might have been, while we entered into another stage of experience.

Without slackening his encircling fingers — as though my arm represented some source of meaning — Gianni embraced me, and I leaned against him. His face, wet with tears shed for Gioconda, was lowered to mine. And when at last we lay down together, his hand, then releasing me, reached up from habit to the back of my head, to grope for the tortoise-shell comb he was accustomed to unclasping there.

"One of the most beautiful novels I have ever read."

**MARK SCHORER**

# THE
# BAY OF
# NOON

## SHIRLEY
## HAZZARD

**PLAYBOY
PAPERBACKS**

The epigraph is taken from W. H. Auden's poem "Good-bye to the Mezzogiorno," which appears in *Homage to Clio*, Random House, Inc., 1960; copyright © 1955, 1956, 1957, 1958, 1959, 1960 by W. H. Auden. Reprinted with permission.

Published simultaneously in the United States and Canada by Playboy Paperbacks, New York, New York. Printed in the United States of America. Library of Congress Catalog Card Number: 81-47257. Reprinted by arrangement with McIntosh & Otis, Inc.

Books are available at quantity discounts for promotional and industrial use. For further information, write to Premium Sales, Playboy Paperbacks, 1633 Broadway, New York, New York 10019.

ISBN: 0-872-16901-4 (U.S.)
   0-872-16963-4 (Canada)

First Playboy Paperbacks printing September 1981. '

*for Francis,*
*and*
*for my Mother*

To bless this region, its vendages, and those
   Who call it home: though one cannot always
Remember exactly why one has been happy,
   There is no forgetting that one was.

W. H. AUDEN
"Good-bye to the Mezzogiorno"

# ❦ I ❧

A MILITARY PLANE crashed that winter on Mount Vesuvius. The plane had taken off from Naples in fog; some hours afterwards, it was reported missing. The search went on for hundreds of miles around — over the Ionian Sea, and at Catania, at Catanzaro. Two days later, when the fog lifted, we could see the wreck quite clearly, crumbled against the snow-streaked cone of the volcano, overlooking the airfield from which it had set out. No one had thought of looking close to home.

Since that time, so they say, we have developed better methods of keeping in touch. For it is twelve or fifteen years, now, since the accident took place.

When I was a child I used to be filled with envy when adults recalled events of twelve or fifteen years before. I would think it must be marvellous, to issue those proclamations of experience — "It was at least ten years ago" or "I hadn't seen him for twenty years." But chronological prestige is tenacious: once attained, it can't be shed; it increases moment by moment, day by day, pressing its honours on you until you are lavishly, overly endowed with them. Until you literally sink under them.

A centenarian has told me that memory protects one from this burden of experience. Whole segments of time dropped out, she said: "Of five or six years, say, around the turn of the century, all I can remember is the dress that someone wore, or the colour of a curtain." And I would be pleased, rather than otherwise, at the prospect of remembering Naples in similar terms — a lilac dress Gioconda wore one morning driving to Caserta, or the Siena-coloured curtains of the apartment in San Biagio dei Librai. But memory, at an interval of only fifteen years, is less economical and less poetic, still clouded with effects and what seemed to be their causes. The search is still under way in unlikely places — too assiduous, too attenuated; too far from home.

There was then, there is still, a big NATO establishment at Naples organized around the United States Sixth Fleet, with token components from other countries. When I was brought there from London to translate documents from Italian into English and to do some clerical sifting and sorting of coloured papers, there were already a number of English girls at the base doing similar things — Angelas and Hilarys and Rosemarys who had wanted to get away from Reading or Ruislip or Holland Park. For the most part those fugitive girls were in their twenties; and over them hung an immanence, a pale expectancy, as if their youth were yet to come to them. What passion they possessed for change had, in getting them to Naples, expended itself; once there, they relapsed into their natural obligingness. Breathlessly polite, they made among the drab or primary colours of military life their tender, uncherished strokes of pastel.

My work, though much like theirs, took place in a different building; my life, while no more nourishing, had been lived on a different continent. I had spent the war out of England. Although I was a child when that took place, there was always an implication to it, if not of defection at least of something regrettable. Even my brother used to say, "Jenny spent the war in Africa," in a way that at once apologised for and excluded me.

I arrived at Naples in autumn, a belatedly inserted item on the budget of a joint mission to study docking and airport facilities with a view to extending them. With a view to extending them, for no such mission ever pronounced the existing state of affairs to be adequate. The airfield — the same airfield that lay to the south, at the foot of the volcano, far from our offices — was to be, for example, enlarged to receive jet planes, which were coming into military use then. In addition, there were rockets, there were higher and higher explosives, there was the prospect of the nuclear submarine. Even in London, where over translations of preliminary papers I learnt the terms I had never in either language known, it seemed implausible that such responsibilities should have devolved on Naples. Ignorant of the Mediterranean, hesitantly speaking an Italian sporadically acquired in Somaliland, I prepared to take the city's part with the loyalty of the native-born.

Our offices were part of a modern complex at Bagnoli, on the northern outskirts of Naples. Modern, I say, but the buildings now have dated in a remarkable way: it is their characterlessness that identifies them, and their resolute unawareness of place. In and around these buildings thousands of NATO personnel and their families lived out their term of exile, requiring nothing of Italy or its language, passing among themselves stale, trumpery talismans of home, recreating a former existence from the shelves of the PX until such time as they should — on other, equally alien shores — speak with nostalgia and authority of the Bay of Naples.

Having arrived with the advance segment of the mission, I was installed along with them — by one of those errors that are the mark of the highly organized — into a hotel in Naples itself, one of the good hotels on the seafront. It was error, then, that set me apart from the first. In the early weeks, when a car fetched us from the hotel before it was light and brought us home each evening after dark, when orders obliged us to idle weekends away in our empty office, we did not live in Naples so much as merely sleep in it. Yet I waited for the city, and its intervention, much in the way that those pale companions of mine awaited life itself.

In the fourth week I was lent — was detailed, as they said, for military precision runs to many syllables — for the day to a British civilian. A marine biologist having letters from Whitehall, he too needed pages translated while he waited for the Naples Aquarium to take him under what my Colonel repeatedly and delightedly called its wing. In the office next to ours a telephone was put down, a name was called. The name was out, sick with a virus; for it, mine was substituted. The following morning I did not take the car — the Vehicle, as the Colonel called it — in the dark to Bagnoli, but walked in winter sunshine the few steps from the Hotel Vesuvio to the Hotel Royal, and sent up my name through the concierge.

Of the morning I remember little: sitting with a pad and pencil in a glassed-in, blue-rugged hotel room — a room that was not, with its aquatic reflections, unlike an aquarium in itself — turning my eyes time and again to the bay; seeing it, because of what I was writing about, not as a blue surface filling a curve of land but as a dense and teeming jungle in which weeds and rocks and wrecks and a million creatures reproduced in strange counterpart the city of Naples itself. Echinoderms, I wrote of, and the Mysidae and the Squillidae, and compiled a list of publications on the Mollusca — these unknowns appearing more familiar in kind than did the accustomed daily litanies of troops and matériel; just as my companion, civil and aloof, seemed more compatible than the sullen hearties of the base. The work went quickly; it was not yet noon when my scientist gave up his silent assembling of the papers that were divided into rows across his bed, and said, "You have caught me up."

With a wad of completed pages in my hand, I rose — to show willing, a sort of coming to attention. He took the finished sheets and put them in a folder without checking them — a courtesy, I thought, like not seeming to count one's change. "Can you go and play for a while? I have to put the next lot together, and something is missing. Could you be back here, say, at three?"

In this way I was set at liberty, and left the hotel as full of joyful purpose as if I had been going to an assignation. Until then I had not been once in the city in the middle of the day. But after weeks of surveillance the sense of freedom came as much from the fact that no one knew where I was, as from walking the seafront of Naples before noon on a fine December morning. The three hours at my disposal — a space of time that now, when all days are my own, often passes unnoticed — seemed then a gift, a luxury beyond which one need not forecast. I did not doubt that I would turn up again at the Hotel Royal at three. The only thing to be thought of was how to spend these hours of one's own.

I possessed a single introduction to Naples — one letter provided by a London acquaintance who had encouraged me to present myself at the address on the envelope. "Somewhere in the thick of Naples," said this well-wisher, who had never himself been there. The address was that of a woman whose name had become known — and was by then becoming forgotten — in connection with one of the post-war films from Italy. There was *Bicycle Thieves,* you remember; there was *Shoeshine,* there was *Open City.* And then there was a film called *Del Tempo Felice* that was made from an obscure little book, a sort of prose poem; and it was the author of this book whose name was on my envelope.

I had never read it, her book. I had seen her film, but I was then very young and had remembered its darkly photographed interiors and flickering close-ups for two reasons — because it was the first time I had been to a film that used sub-titles; and the first time that I saw the lines of Dante from which the title was taken and which appeared, off-centre, on the screen along with the other credits, duly translated in sub-title but carrying, as sometimes happens, in their own, then unfamiliar language, the physical aspect of poetry that sends a shiver across the sight and skin.

And now that there was time to call myself to her attention, I could only think: a woman of this kind, with work, friends, admirers — a public, even — would hardly welcome a stranger with no better credentials than a note (a note which I had seen for myself began "Dear Signorina") from a remote acquaintance at Ealing Studios.

The name — her Christian name, that is — had struck

me; also the address, for there was a street number, then simply "San Biagio dei Librai": Saint Biagio of the Booksellers. I had remarked on this address when the letter was handed to me. And the friend at Ealing — who had known the lady, it now came out, only outside Italy — said, "Let's hope I got it right. I rather gather this is the good old family palazzo. I hope she'll do you proud." All had, in fact, been in the realm of aspiration or surmise.

It occurred to me, as I walked back to the Hotel Vesuvio, that I might telephone this Signorina at once and see if she would have me. But the prospect of picking up the telephone and shattering her unsuspecting morning was more than I could face for her; and when I got up to my room I took out, instead of her address, a guidebook that had lain one month in the bureau drawer.

"The traveller who would know Naples" — so the guidebook dictated, open on the hotel counterpane — "must take himself to Spaccanápoli, the split of Naples, the street that traversed the city's nucleus in classical times, and is now called San Biagio dei Librai."

Nevertheless it took some time to make the call. First I got cut off, and in the wire a low voice asked, though not of me, "*Tu, come giudici?*" Then I heard the telephone ringing, ringing, and was about to hang up at the instant when the ringing exchanged itself for a voice. Tracing the hotel's stitched monogram with a nervous finger, I made myself known; and in English the voice cried, "Good. Good that you called. Yes, come, come. Come now. Come for lunch. Are you coming in a taxi? — my street is up, you can't enter, it's the drains. Tell him to let you out at the Gesù Nuovo, the church. Then ask the way, it's only a few minutes on foot from there."

Below the Gesù Nuovo there is a ramp of a street that rises to a corner where Degas once lived with his Neapolitan relatives. The ascent, oblique, suggests the piazza above by giving, as if through a door ajar on a high landing, a glimpse of the exorbitant, gem-cut façade of a church, with to the left a flash of red stucco, to the right an ornate obelisk, before it catapults you on to a scene that appears, from this method of approaching it, more bizarre than ever.

Had I been accompanied, I might have laughed out loud at the profligacy of imagination expended there; but solitude, which is held to be a cause of eccentricity, in fact imposes excessive normality, at least in public, and I crossed the piazza with no outward sign of interest and placed myself against the faceted stones of the church. From there one looked, then, across at the bombed shell of Santa Chiara, half-reconstructed, and at a derelict campanile on the one hand and a massive palace on the other; and this I did for some moments, only showing it was new to me by enquiring, of the priest who came to close the church, the way to San Biagio dei Librai.

The day had deteriorated, it was winter again, and the piazza was abandoned for the siesta. One pre-war Fiat, as lonely, as historic as the single car on an antiquated postcard, had been parked in the middle of the square. And I, perhaps, walking away from the church door, would have something now of the same anonymous, arrested look — captured, as the saying goes, in the picture; serving to show, merely, by human contrast, the dimensions of buildings, to date the photograph unwittingly with my clothes and hair; somebody purloined from a crowd to act as an example. The light itself had dwindled to the joyless sepia of an old photograph.

The picture is re-animated — rather, it dissolves to life — and I enter a passageway of a street, the narrow channel that flows out from the farther side of the square. Past a hundred shops and stalls that sold, as they are selling still, song records, coloured nylon sponges, the gauze and sugar paraphernalia of christenings and first communions, plastic Bambis, bolts of print material, gold jewellery and silver representations of arms and legs to be offered up to departmental saints; past open sacks of coffee beans, stacks of books new and seventh-hand, and barrows piled with hand-tools — through this I came, that afternoon, into San Biagio dei Librai. What could be closed was closing in a savage drum-roll of descending grilles; what could be wheeled was being trundled away. Over cobbled blocks — that were posted here and there with stone bollards intended to keep out the cars that expertly slid between them and rushed on to straddle a long trench of drainage repairs — I walked by palaces of stone and stucco, rusticated or red, white with grey facings, brown, orange, rose or ochre, no two alike, facing each other across the street's corridor as monumentally as if they had been rising, isolated, in some open place that did their proportions justice.

On to the flanks of those palaces, smaller buildings had been grafted in every age except our own — in any unlikely opening, on any precarious ledge, apparently with the sole provision that they bear no resemblance to one another. Forgotten or overlaid, antiquity had been buried in the walls, making its laconic signal — a sunken column, Greek, dark, smooth as silk, with acanthus capital; a Roman inscription, traces of a fortification, or crenellations that, centuries since, had been surmounted by a rooftop. In one vast courtyard was planted a colossal sculpture, Roman or Renaissance, of a horse's head; another ended in galleries of disintegrating frescoes.

It was a deep square of a building, hers; pale stucco, divided into a dozen apartments, or a hundred. The *portiere*, coming out from his lunch with his fork, spooled with pasta, in his hand, directed me to the piano nobile, taking me into the courtyard to point out, in a fold of that flaking parchment, the inner staircase I should take. There were several flights of deep stone steps, unlit, uncarpeted. Only on the last landing, in the spot where one paused to draw breath before ringing the bell, an oblong of shredding crimson had been placed before a pair of dark doors and carried dusty, tapering impressions of several days' shoes.

I rang the bell, heard nothing, rang again. The excitement of the street receded. Anticlimax brought back the sense of intrusion, as I stood there with the letter in my handbag like a warrant to search, to root out secrets.

From far off, as if it had been beyond the building, a woman's voice called, "Tosca!" There was silence, there was movement, and the same voice calling, "Tosca, Tosca." The voice approached the door, so full and musical that it might have been introducing an aria. A bolt was drawn, a handle rattled, and the dark door opened.

Gioconda's appearance has become merged now with knowledge of her, with moods and events and questions, so that in describing it I feel I am giving a false impression and introducing, even to myself, a woman I do not know. If one says that she was rather tall, dark-haired, dark-eyed, with in winter a pale colouring, paler than apricot, one has described nothing more than a woman who is in all probability good-looking. Even in giving these few facts I am getting off the track, for I myself would hardly recognise her from such a description: it is almost as if I were describing her skeleton, without the intercostal tissue that gave it life and singularity. Yet her physical beauty was as strong a part of her character as though she were personally accountable for the deep setting of the eyes or the long rise of the cheekbone. Its first and lasting impression was one of vitality and endurance. That is to say, of power: a power as self-contained, as unoppressive as that of a splendid tree.

In haste she had pulled both doors apart, and stood for an instant with a hand raised along each of them. A coiled weight of hair was prefigured in the upward, backward carriage of the head. She wore a sweater of some dark colour, and a flannel skirt divided into pleats as was then the fashion, and round her feet a heavy white cat was making the figure eight.

As we greeted one another and she stood aside, tripping the cat, to let me enter, Tosca — presumably it was Tosca — appeared at last from the furthest corner of a dim hallway and stood for a moment there like a figure barely discerned in the background of some dark canvas — a presence made mysterious, perhaps, simply by the fact that it is indistinct.

Gioconda brought me into a high room closed off from light and air by outer and inner shutters, and by the custom of southern cities unalterable on the coldest days; smelling of wax, of winter, of mildew and precautions against mildew. The walls were darkly red, narrowly banded at floor level with grey and topped with a two-foot frieze of a grey geometrical design whose regularity was flawed here and there by age or damp. There were thick curtains, thin carpets, worn velvet chairs and footstools. There were pictures, and a mesh-fronted bookcase of bound books paired with a glass-fronted cabinet of porcelain. Two small sofas were ranged by an immense cold fireplace that, like a dormant Vesuvius, presided over everything.

I took note, that first time, of all these fittings and fixtures I was never to notice again; imagining them, then, to have some bearing on her life as I was to know it. But she led me through the room as if it had been no more than a passage, into a small study filled with light and littered with papers and books. Plants and vases, pencils and matchboxes had arranged themselves there with a look of purposeful incongruity, like objects for still-life grouped about an artist's studio. The windows were unshuttered, and a maltreated Empire desk, from which some of the bronzes were missing, stood between them. There was a cushioned chair, in bad shape, on which the cat at once circled itself; and a striped divan on which we sat, she and I, speechless and inquisitive like children at first school.

"So here you are," said Gioconda, as if she had been awaiting my arrival for a long time — or as if, entering into my own point of view, she could regard my presence in her room as the fulfilment of an intention, even though not her own. It was curious to think, then, how I had for weeks been aware of her, while she had not known of my existence.

"Your street," I said to her. "Your street is marvellous."

"Oh — this street . . ." She thought so too — so much so that good manners called for her to depreciate it. "They're always telling me — my friends — Why don't you move? Because it's rough round here, you know, a kind of important squalor."

"Not squalor exactly —"

"Not squalor!" she cried. "If this street isn't squalor, I'd like to know what is." We both laughed at her indignation, she putting her hand up to her mouth in a gesture so completely hers that the picturing of it brings her more before my eyes than any photograph could do — it was as if she were, quite irrationally, self-conscious about her mouth or her teeth, or unavailingly wished to be more moderate in her responses. "This is Naples with a vengeance — and literally so, since we have the vendetta round here: I'm always hearing the grocer was stabbed, or that they're on the lookout for the dry-cleaner. But there it is — it's what I'm used to, I couldn't live elsewhere." Saying this, her expression clouded, as if being bound to that place was a disturbing rather than a stabilising attachment. "I was born here." She turned to me and asked, again as if we were children exchanging information, "Where were you born?"

It isn't so much where one was born (as a matter of fact, in my case, it was in Notting Hill Gate), but what one remembers. I told Gioconda how, as a child, I had been sent with other children on a ship to Cape Town to escape the Blitz. How my mother died at the end of the war and my brother came out to Africa to work in

Somaliland, and I moved there with him, and at last went back to London.

"London is nice," she said. "I was there not so long ago. We'll talk about it another day, when there's more time."

This assumption of our friendship moved me, in my loneliness, with a sort of joy — that this lovely, vital creature was to attach her life, however lightly, to mine. I was touched, but showed no pleasure — just as when I had stood in the Piazza del Gesù, and walked under the windows of San Biagio dei Librai. In fact I was often, later on, to act out with Gioconda a circumspection I did not feel: her abundance made others reticent; her openness evoked discretion.

"I'm called Jenny," I told her, in answer to her question — for we were pursuing our child-like exchange, as if we might at any moment have come out with "How old are you?" or "What does your father do?"

"It's not your name, then?"

"Jenny is a bureaucratic accident. My name is Penelope. When I was put on board the ship for South Africa at the beginning of the war, I was called Penny. But there were so many of us — so many little Mollies and Timmies and Patties — that the woman in charge of us got the names mixed up. Jenny was as close as she ever came to mine. I was not of an age to make an issue of it. I went on board as Penny and disembarked as Jenny."

Gioconda said nothing — imagining, I knew, the journey. Whenever the matter came up, people expressed anguish over that uprooting of mine. Yet — although the sufferings of children are the worst, being inextinguishable — children themselves seldom have a proper sense of their own tragedy, discounting and keeping hidden the true horrors of their short lives, humbly imagining real calamity to be some prestigious drama of the grown-up world. Other, unconfided things were worse to me, at the time, than the actual fact of my removal to South Africa — for that searing displacement at least bore official sanction in the minds of adults and was shared with hundreds of others. The loss of my name, and for such a reason, did not offend me until much later; indeed — for even a child can wish for the illusion of a new identity, arriving in a strange country, purged of the past, starting afresh; in fact a child is more entitled to the delusion — I fancied, as I landed at Cape Town, that the voyage was enabling me to begin what, with no sense of comedy, I identified to myself as a new life. A double life, rather, for in my letters and my homesickness I remained Penny. As a little girl, however, I saw myself as such, insignificant in the convulsions of war, and believed I had no cause for complaint in a world where soldiers died and cities were devastated. It is only in retrospect I know myself to have been among the victims of war, and dare not mention that at the time I suffered, more grotesquely, over exclusion from a school party, or from the fear of punishment in connection with a torn blazer.

That stranded childhood comes back to me in curious ways, with unlikely associations. The sea, for instance — in those years of war children were greatly aware of the sea and of those imperilled on it. It was the ocean, its impassability, that lay between me and the natural course of my life; between me and home. The ships of my childhood figured like heroes in their disasters — the *City of Benares*, the *Jervis Bay*, the *San Demetrio*, the *Ark Royal*, the *Graf Spee*. We used to see ships, shabby, painted grey, put in at Cape Town harbour, to disappear in the night and perhaps forever. We knew their shapes and tonnages, we accumulated stories of the Atlantic crossings and the Arctic convoys. We knew that the Queens could outpace any U-boat and carried eight thousand troops, and that you could stay fourteen days in a neutral port. By contrast it seems now that the sea has almost retired from our lives, and that ships are leading a marginal, twilight existence, like senior officials who resist being pensioned off.

Gioconda said, "Yet I think you look more like Jenny than Penelope. I could never picture Penelope with that colour hair."

"Sometimes, though, I still feel like Penelope. When I fill out a form, it feels appropriate." I remarked on her own name.

"It is not uncommon in Italy. Or common either." The cat, she said, completing the game of names, was called Iocasta: had been thus renamed, from Innocente, after conceiving kittens with its own son. In commendation or sympathy she snatched it up — round the middle, with both hands, as a child might — gave it a squeeze and set it down again on its chair, where it smoothly resumed a wash interrupted in mid-lick. "Come on to the terrace and tell me if it's warm enough to lunch out there."

That room of hers gave on to a terrace, long and wide and sheltered at one end by a pergola draped with the wintry skeletons of vines and by wistaria that still showed, here and there, a purple tassel or a frond of green. At the other end there were stone boxes of marigolds. A table had been laid for us in the pale sun, and one of its legs was lengthened with a wedge of paper to meet the uneven tiles.

"It's heaven," I said. We leant on the balustrade and looked down. On the opposite side of the cortile there were two or three small businesses — a woodworker's, a printer's giving out a clackety rhythm, and a narrow archway marked "*Autoscuola.*"

"Yes, truly, it's a garage, a driving school." Gioconda's hand went to her mouth. "I suppose you qualify for the licence if you can get the car out of this courtyard."

It was not, after all, the good old family palazzo. Her father had owned a larger part of it until the war. "What I have now — they made an entrance, broke up the enfilade of main rooms — it's just what you've seen, with another room or two . . . The thing was to keep this."

She meant the terrace, patting the stone railing with the flat of her hand.

She still had relatives in Naples — "too many by far" — but they were cousins and second cousins. She had a sister she was fond of, much older, who lived at Nice. "Luciana. She married a Frenchman. Before the war. He was killed in '44." She broke off to lead me to the end of the terrace. "From here you can see everything."

It was almost true, this everything, for the arches and towers and polychrome domes were stacked there beside and behind each other like so much scenery backstage at a theatre, all painted by Monsù Desiderio. There was no tracing the streets that unrolled like ribbons among them, no accounting for the cloisters and vast gardens that appeared at intervals, like optical illusions in the foreshortened scene — the congested, backstage effect heightened by the fact that we were looking into the city and away from the sea. There was no outlook, in any usual sense; except to our left where, painted by a different hand, a segment of the Vomero rose up in tiers of fields and buildings.

"That red curve of houses follows the wall of the theatre where Nero sang." The big thing below the cathedral had been a paleo-Christian temple. Those columns came from a temple of the Dioscuri, that church was the site of the Roman basilica. The question "What is it?" took on, here, an aspect of impertinence; one might only learn what it had successively been.

Gioconda told me that San Biagio was the patron saint of throats; little children prayed to him about their tonsils, he had an attraction for singers with laryngitis. I recalled a variety of labral discs among the silver offerings on sale in the street, and knew these, now, to be throats.

When we sat down to our lunch, she asked me, "How did you arrive in Italy?" and I told her how I had been flown to Milan with my military men for a conference there, and sent on by train. I was grateful to her for mentioning the journey. At that time, when the mere idea that I was, for example, on the Lombardy Plain could keep me enchanted through mile after mile of level countryside, the excitement of entering Italy had gone undivulged. And I enumerated the farms and castles and cities that lay along the length of Italy as if she herself had never known of them.

She filled our glasses, and said, "I hope you'll be happy here," as though she were responsible. That struck her too, for she remarked, "I talk like a landlady who is taking in a new lodger."

I told her I had seen nothing of Naples until that day, how it had come about that I was free to telephone her, and I looked at my watch. At once she asked when I could come again. I had to go to the airport on an errand the following Friday afternoon, and I said I could drop in on the way back.

"Yes, of course, come, come," she said, as she had on

the telephone. "Friday, a friend arrives . . . from Rome. He'll be so pleased to meet you."

I wondered if it were the friend of so many photographs — in her room, on the desk, on the mantelpiece, ranged on a low bookcase; snapshots of a white, sunburnt smile on a stony beach, of muscular legs in shorts climbing a cliff-face, or bare arms tensed to suspend a heavy fish on a hook; one foot placed on a step or a rock, one hand bracing the trunk of a confident tree. The name she now said was new to me; though her glance, tentative, enquiring, might have suggested otherwise. I thought, the map of her existence is soon to be flagged, for me, with these encampments and shrines, these centres of interest; and again the notion gave pleasure.

When I got up to go, she held out her hand. She surprised me by asking, "What is he like, your biologist?"

"He's a Scotsman."

"A sandy, bristly little chap, then?"

"Not at all. Lean, dark, restrained. Like a furled umbrella."

"When he speaks, can one tell that he's from Scotland?"

"Sometimes. Some words quite a bit."

"What's his name?"

"Tulloch. J. P. Tulloch. That's all I know." This Neapolitan curiosity infected me, though, for in answering it I brought out more than I thought I knew. I said, "He reminds me of my brother."

# ❧ II ❧

My brother's wife is an emphatic little woman. When I first knew her, she could look delicious even so, an infuriated kitten. "Oh, it's outrageous," she would say, flashing neat little teeth in her rage. "One has to take a stand." Or "I don't have to put up with this sort of thing." And I would agree: "Absolutely," I'd say, or "Absolutely not," according to the occasion, not caring, not even hearing, but looking emphatic too, just to please. Just to please, not Norah, but my brother.

At the end of the war, when I might have expected to return to my relatives in London, they prevailed on me instead to stay in South Africa to finish grammar school. England then was no place, it was agreed among them, for me or for anybody — no visible end to the rationing of food, the shortage of fuel, the lack of every comfort and of some necessities. My mother came out to South Africa to see me, during the terrible English winter of 1947. I had grown up without her, and now I was old enough to be touched by what I recognised in her as the ravages of war. She was exhausted, from sleepless nights, from fearing death, from longing for me and grieving for others, from standing in queues and mending old clothes. It showed in her distinctly, it would set her apart at once from others in a Cape Town street, even though she was an ordinary, fair, little woman. She wasn't unlike my sister-in-law to look at, as a matter of fact — though Norah used to be glamorous, which my mother never was. But my mother didn't have that emphatic quality of Norah's either, or those reserves of antagonism that generate the energy for working out one's will.

My mother died suddenly a few months after her return to London. She had been too much depleted. During her last days at Cape Town I remember plying her with extra nourishment and setting her in the sun, as if she were a shrivelled plant one was attempting to coax back to life. They wrote me, "Her heart gave out" — her heart that had, I suppose, been giving out always, to everybody, with no revitalising intake of grievances or self-pity. For some time after that it seemed I could not urge reconsideration of my future — a future that was being consumed in its very abeyance: they had too much on their hands, must not be asked to think about more; so I reasoned, as if I had no existence other than as an extra item for someone else's consideration, a potential last straw. There was a lot of such abnegation among young people then — we lived as a foil for the concerns of our elders. When I was told that in another year, a year or two, I would be sent for, I simply began to put that time behind me. Time is said to seem long to the young, but it is only the young who can be so prodigal of it, looking forward to far-off events and wishing away the intervening weeks or months as if they were no more than an impediment to a goal.

When, eventually, recall was settled on, it was not easy to get passage. And the same week that the ticket was written out by the Shaw Savill Line, my brother cabled me to stay where I was, for he was coming out to Africa. He had taken a post as an irrigation engineer in Italian Somaliland, as we called it then, with a new development agency, and the idea now was that I should go with him to Mogadiscio and keep house there.

And so it happened that I spent three years on the coast of East Africa before at last I came home to England — more, as my father (remarried now, and keeping clear, in Yorkshire) remarked, like Ulysses than Penelope.

It was when my brother married Norah that I came back. Edmund had been recalled from Somalia to London in connection with a possible promotion. During his absence I ran our little house, did some typing for an import-export firm, and saw the few people we were in the habit of seeing. When I was asked about my brother's return, I would say, "Very soon" or "Any day," believing I had the information to give. All this time, change was heading for me unapprehended, like a torpedo or a crocodile: while I was typing out somebody's invoice, or going to the beach in someone's Land Rover, or fishing the wedge of orange out of my Pimm's Cup, Edmund was taking Norah to the pictures, or to see the London production of *South Pacific*, or kissing her goodnight (for couples, in those days, still did kiss goodnight) in the hallway of her parents' house in S.W.7 after a family Sunday of roast lamb and denunciation of Sir Stafford Cripps. When Edmund decided to remain in England, it was assumed that I too would settle there — just as it had earlier been assumed that I would stay with him in Africa. I don't know why it was taken for granted; like so many arrangements that should have been contested, it was described as a foregone conclusion.

Returning to England had lost its initial meaning and taken on another. If it could no longer assuage a home-sickness that, after its heart-splitting genesis in childhood exile, had not so much abated as become a permanent sense of lack, it gave, in compensation, unlooked-for, adult pleasures. It pleased me, for instance, that the plants and seasons now corresponded to literature; that Nature was not the sole index of age; that the rewards of one's surroundings were rendered in architecture, rather than in the unearned prestige of Table Mountain.

I did not live with Norah and Edmund. But digs were found for me near their first flat in Sloane Avenue, and now I partook of their own Sunday lamb, served up on wedding presents, while Norah described to me her plans for carpets and curtains, or showed me the sample of bedspread material she had hung over a chair to see if she could live with it. When I began to know her, I wondered if their courtship had been, for her, something of the same — my brother draped over a chair for the statutory length of time, to see if she could live with him. In that case she might have noticed that he did not really go with the surroundings; perhaps she did see this, but knew that he would fade to a better match.

To me it was quite incredible that they should be married and have a private life of lovemaking, of confidences exchanged and silences shared, of bills and latchkeys — their personalities converged so little and so seldom. Even Norah's married name, Norah Unsworth, struck one as unlikely, the two blurred vowels coming together awkwardly and the whole sounding as if it belonged to the heroine of a schoolgirl's story.

The thing was, my brother adored her. That was the great and touching thing. The strength of his passion had somehow carried them both through the forms of betrothal and marriage, and continued to make a synthesis of their disparate personalities. He did not require of her that she be sympathetic to him, or intelligent about others: it was enough for her to sit there on one of those cretonne-covered chairs, holding up her Minton cup and saucer, for him to feel satisfied with his choice. For her part, Norah showed no more curiosity about Edmund than she did about anyone else — never asking his opinion or encouraging him to reveal himself; but she too was borne along by her effect on him — it was as if the active force of his love kept her upright on her flowered chair and stabilised the cup in her hand, like some proposition in physics. She was exceedingly pretty, with fair, silky hair that hung straight down like Joan of Arc's, and fine little features. Her skin was pale, but she had vivid pink cheeks and would refer to "my English complexion," as if she might have had some other kind. (Only her hands were strangely broad and strong, with a vehement, wrenching grip; as a fat woman will have trim, delicate feet, so did fragile Norah have these masterful large wrists and grasping fingers.)

Girls are not now described as dainty, but dainty was the word for Norah. Edmund loved to look at her: I had not realised, in Africa, how much he felt the lack of England.

At the same time, he had still, then, other requirements. That was where I came in — literally, since I took to coming in as often as they asked me and supplying missing links. It was not that my brother and I talked about our own concerns in Norah's presence, but there was always the silent assumption that I would overlook Norah's triviality and would go on wadding up, around her little speeches of censure and self-centredness, enough indulgence to absorb them. And this made it appear, for a time, as if Edmund and I were in league with one another, not against Norah but in her favour;

almost as though he and I were the married couple, and
she some third party whom we had agreed to humour.

I have never spent so much time with a being who had
no interest beyond herself. Norah talked a lot about
human relationships, as she called them (for she had
picked up some kind of jargon and was always saying
"identify" and "communicate," could scarcely look at
Edmund and me without the word "siblings" popping
out), but spoke as if these were a special subject, like
lepidoptery or tropical plants, of which one could hardly
hope to encounter interesting examples in daily life.

Like many English people she passionately wished to
attach herself to the well-born and well-known. Adulation
of the royal family was too commonplace for her, and
she had amassed instead a great deal of information on
fashionable life, from magazines and newspapers. Once
in a while, at some large cocktail party or benefit performance, her life did glancingly touch this coveted
sphere, and it was as if she spent the long intervals pre-
paring for such moments. She had never been to Cap
Ferrat or Corfu, but knew who had villas there and where
one ought to stay. She could tell you which Honourable
Amanda was going with what younger son, and how the
parents felt about it. As a scholar might value some
revelation that extended his concept, so did she receive
the discovery that the Belvoir Hunt was pronounced
"Beaver," or that the name Leveson-Gower should be
said "Looson-Gore"; her joy in such details was the

measure of her relief at the revelatory gaffe she had been spared.

She clung to these social canons and cyphers as desperately as if she had been raised among anarchists.

With all this went an obsession for getting behind the scenes, being shown over by someone in the know. With her I went to television stations, to film sets, to tea on the terrace at Westminster — and even, once, up narrow stairs and down long corridors to the board room at Paddington Station, a large white oblong containing, like one of those oriental sets of diminishing boxes, a green baize oblong only slightly less large, and lined with huge, faded photographs of locomotives with names like the *Windsor Castle* and the *Lancashire Witch*.

One day, poor Norah, she would get behind the scenes once and for all, lost for good. Only my brother's patient love drew her out by its thread, time after time, from those labyrinthine inner circles where she sought to invest herself with the trappings of authority or of social standing; to enter a company to which she felt herself — perhaps rightly — entirely qualified to belong.

They were an odd lot, Norah and her family. No, that's not it — they weren't odd enough, and that's the truth. They belonged to the pre-war British middle class that feels itself in ambush in this world; were full of the petty derelictions of the neighbours, the local legends of bad deeds. They had no friend whom they did not, in absence, constantly and treacherously deride.

They suspected *me* of being odd, and tried to settle me down, down, with bachelors from their own circle. These young men also existed in a continual state of righteous exasperation, saying things like "That could have been foreseen," and being "fed to the teeth." They were of that type described by Gogol, men who "itch to maintain discipline everywhere and to enforce their views on station-masters and cabmen." One of them, I remember, wrote a letter to *The Times* urging that Teddy-boys be "firmly suppressed."

Yet decency nagged at their reluctant hearts; and they acknowledged that, too, in unconscious phrases — "I fail to understand . . .," "I cannot bring myself to overlook . . .," "Tolerance is all very well up to a point . . ." — as if they had tried the ways of magnanimity but found them too exigent.

If this was an aspect of the England I had left, it was by no means the one to which I most wished to return.

We put up with our state of affairs, Edmund, Norah, and I, for nearly three years; I suppose that is a short time, really, for it is in the nature of such things to go on for a lifetime. For a while Edmund truly welcomed it because, as long as I would complement his marriage, it was a happy, even an ideal, one. Like other persons who are described as weak, he rigorously commanded protective services from others. Norah put up with it because she enjoyed having me to patronise, and having those requirements of Edmund's — humour, curiosity — that she could not meet supplied by me; in the way that a frigid wife might have unconsciously encouraged her husband to take a mistress. And I put up with it because I was in love with my brother.

In the telling, it is obvious. In the telling, all things are. If one says that one was young at the time, that alters nothing. One is always something, after all, at the time: one is old, one is young, one is in love, or in trouble, or poor or over-worked. It does not much matter what the extenuating circumstance is, and youth is mentioned here merely as the key to this particular piece of obtuseness.

It was when this love dawned on me — as it literally did, one grey sunrise, while I stood at my window looking at the brick backs of the houses on the Fulham Road — that Edmund began to wish me away; in becoming aware, I had outlived my usefulness. Now he must go on, take different measures, take a mistress, collect stamps, stay late at the office. It was then that I resigned from my job at Pascoe and Wingrove (Norah's father's firm), and applied to be sent to Naples.

# ❧ III ❧

It was a surprise, after Gioconda's photographs, to have her friend appear fully, even heavily, clothed, in a worn camel's-hair coat and a blue woollen scarf. Yet there was in Gianni's attitude, as he appeared in her doorway a moment after my own arrival, so much of the triumphant, fish-catching stance that I should truly have known him anywhere. Though his face, with high forehead and high-bridged nose and expressive contours, was that of a city person, there was an athletic proficiency about his body. There were always certain borderline aspects to Gianni's style: his proud walk might, on a bad day, almost have been called a strut; his litheness was the professional grace of someone who keeps himself in what is called "condition."

Gianni, then, was forty-eight years old.

At once I found myself mildly resenting, on Gioconda's behalf, the way in which he made himself at home. I had understood he was Gioconda's lover (that very evening it was made known to me that he was separated from his wife and could not get an annulment); but he took satisfaction in making this clear, as if I had been a rival for her affections. Letting Tosca, who was half his height, take his coat, he asked her what there was for dinner. In no time he was making drinks for us on the marble-topped chest that served as the bar, unerringly reaching — as he turned his head to talk to me — for the right bottle, or placing his hand on a dish of lemons. If something was in his way he moved it without hesitation — chucking a magazine on to the sofa, dumping a pot of cyclamens on Gioconda's blotter. While these confident gestures were not quite made for one's benefit, it was evident that Gianni enjoyed the resolute exercise of his limbs and the accurate, unapologetic placing of his well-shod feet on the earth. I slouched more than ever into my chair in defiance of his good example. In a way I liked watching it, all the same.

As I was to learn, it was not hard to entertain Gianni; for he loved to talk about himself. In a world populated, as he never tired of illustrating, by *cretini* and *analfabeti* Gianni always triumphed, one gathered, with crushing ripostes or by reckless action. The catalogue of his victories was like a comic-strip serial, always following the same pattern: Gianni, intrepid, took arms against envy, stupidity, or cowardice, and routed them. The forces of envy, stupidity and cowardice, endlessly returning, were endlessly put to flight. Bulletins of the campaign were interspersed with accounts of the gratitude of fair women, of feats of physical strength, or of the manifestly misplaced confidences of the celebrated. A lot of this was funny stuff, and the whole made tolerable by the same stylish self-assertion that showed in Gianni's bearing and gestures.

Nevertheless, watching him that first day in Gioconda's room, I wondered how she put up with him.

Later, when I saw more of Gianni, his attraction for Gioconda was to become more of a puzzle. Where Gianni was concerned it was as if she forfeited her critical faculties — at least I could not tell what she made of his boasting and his magisterial ways. He liked, for instance, to humiliate Gioconda in small things — "Your nails need doing" or "It turns out you were quite wrong about . . ." — but when, once or twice, I protested these remarks and took Gioconda's part, she herself upheld him, saying, "Well, he's right after all" or "I must have got it wrong, then," and Gianni would give me a smug glance, like a child that has scored over another child with the grown-ups.

He would even, at his worst, lead her on, encouraging her to speak of some incident or impression in order to demolish all the more conclusively her point of view; or her affectionate mood would be developed so that it might be all the more grossly ruptured: he was kind, in fact, in order to be cruel.

The likeable side of Gianni was inextricable from all this, and made itself felt in flashes of directness or practicality that gave an idea of how he conducted his work. For Gianni made films, and it was Gianni who had directed the film made from Gioconda's book: in this way they had met. There was a compensating generosity in his nature that would rush in to fill the cavities gouged out by his own unkindness. Unexpectedly he would remember some interest you had expressed, or some small object admired in a window would turn up for you in his pocket. The mention of an injury you had suffered would instantly have him crying down the imbecile who had offered it — and in this respect he was a true friend, never once indulging the fiction that there are two sides to every question.

That first evening when we had our drinks and I got up to go, it was his generosity — and I think, too, a sense of not having been a success with me — that moved him to take me by the hand and ask me to spend the following day with them; for the Colonel had given me, for the first time, a Saturday free.

"We're trying out my new car," Gianni said. "Driving to Herculaneum, and on to Sorrento for lunch. Gioconda, tell her to come."

Gioconda looked pleased, as if he did not always approve her friends. "What a good idea. Of course."

"There you are. You must." Gianni let go of my hand. "It's a Maserati."

At the front door I said to Gioconda, who had come to let me out, "It's kind, but I won't."

"If you're free, why ever not?"

"Because this is your time together." I had learnt that Gianni came at weekends, and drove back to Rome on Sunday evenings.

"Oh, if it's only that —" Now Gioconda took my hand, as Gianni had done, and then released it. I was reminded of how she had quickly squeezed the cat. "We'll pick you up at ten, say."

"But can you bear to have me there? When you might be alone together?"

Gioconda considered this, then said reasonably, "Of course I could not bear it if, at the end of the day, it was you who were to go to bed with him." She laughed at my surprise as she closed the door. "About ten, then."

On my way back to the hotel I bought a bunch of yellow roses from a stand in Via Santa Lucia. A strong, gritty wind had blown up, and it snatched out of my hand the fragments of change I had been given. The five- and ten-lire pieces came, then, in wrinkled miniature banknotes instead of coins, and two or three of these wheeled about the footpath, creating false opulence around me and giving desperate exercise to a group of urchins with fierce, elderly faces. When I unwrapped the roses in my room, I found I had been given only the broken heads of flowers, discards of some florist; but these had been fixed to their false stems with such patient professionalism — so intricately wired and laced, so ingeniously sheathed in green — that one seemed almost to have profited from the deception. They lasted few days, these ironic flowers of Naples, though perhaps as long as any roses at that season.

The same evening I wrote to my brother, "All the bananas in Italy are from Somaliland. Every day, somewhere, I pass a stall of Somali bananas — the fruits, quite literally, of your labours." When I wrote this sort of thing to Edmund I had to wonder if I were not excluding Norah, still invoking the existence that Edmund and I had once shared. Yet — so I thought — it might be as well to leave them a little something to put up with: I knew, and the knowledge gave pain, how often Edmund would assure himself that my disappearance was the best thing for everyone concerned — it is what people always say when they have arranged something exclusively to suit themselves. If he no longer wanted to learn about himself, why should I assist in that deception? In Africa I had been young enough to enjoy my influence over him without recognising that it originated in his weakness.

This reasoning covered the wish to hurt him. But resentment begets perception, of a kind, and the reason itself was true — the part about Edmund's not wishing to know himself. He was catching slogans from Norah and, if he did ever speak of his own character now, it was to inter it in a heap of abstractions. "I'm something of a masochist," he would write me, as casually as he might have said, "I've joined the Athenaeum"; or "I'm in my

manic phase." Thus, gratefully, he renounced unique-
ness for a textbook anonymity. "That's just people" had
become his favourite phrase.

His opinions too had taken on much of Norah. She put
words into his mouth; and they emerged, lightly coloured like litmus paper by his own mild reaction.

The habit of meeting Edmund's requirements was
strong in me, all the same, and my letters home were in
general as bland as the replies that came back. "I have
been befriended here by an Italian woman . . . ," thinking as I wrote how Norah and her circle, with their con-
ventional anglicised idea of all south Italy, would imagine Gioconda, if they imagined her at all — picturing
her squat, voluble, perhaps with a light moustache. I
even played up, involuntarily, to this misconception — it
is useless to offer true impressions of one's life to those
who actively desire not to learn of it in other than un-
troublesome terms; one might as well subscribe to whatever fiction is imposed. Beyond this was the instinct, of
self-preservation, to keep this tentative new existence to
myself.

My sister-in-law's letters were vehement in their wish
to forestall any suggestion of infelicity on my part. If
this was to be the best thing for everyone, there was to be
no possibility of second thoughts. "Good to know you are
so happy," she would say in every letter. Assiduously
she built up a climate into which the realities of a life as
formless and solitary as mine could never intrude. "You

must be very happy," she would direct me; "I tell everyone how happy you are," she would warn, producing witnesses. These letters arrived without mercy at every crisis of my life, and they do so still.

On the other hand, she got edgy if, compliantly, I spoke of genuine pleasure. When I wrote of the white steamers setting out for Capri, she replied, "Capri must be very spoilt now." If I mentioned the streets of Naples, she wrote back, "I can never forget that American gangsterism originated there." My smallest achievement must be minimised: "Lucky you." With Norah the unconscious was always uppermost: you had to dig down to find the conscious.

Of true homesickness — the longing for the habitual — I suffered little, for I had never acquired or been provided with familiar things; mine, from childhood, had been an existence improvised among the unfamiliar. Nothing, in those first weeks at Naples, could seem as deeply alien as that life of indignation and Sunday roasts that I had left behind. For my brother, however, and our lost companionship, our lost intimacy of thought and look and word, I suffered what one does for love, assailed — in a shop or at my desk, while continuing to talk of other things — by anguish, as by the pang of some mortal but concealed infirmity. A postcard from Edmund, sent to me from Stockholm where he had briefly gone on business, moved me to desolate tears — so separate did we seem from one another then, each in a place unimaginable to the other, each irrevocably set on his tangential course, the dividing ocean once more between us . . . *O Seigneur, que tant de mers me séparent de vous.*

Nonetheless I knew, hating to know it, that our condition was not the worst, since one of us wished it that way. It is when both desire it otherwise that logic is violated, and the course of events seems uselessly, fatally, distinguished from the will.

# ❧ IV ❧

GIANNI SANG. He sang rather well, and quite a lot. When very young he had the idea of becoming a professional singer, but abandoned it because of the battles one had to fight. There were the teachers, the impresarios who did not recognise talent, or were jealous of it; there was the now celebrated cellist who, auditioning together with the youthful Gianni, had talked throughout Gianni's performance.

"*Dunque* — '*Maestro*,' I asked him. 'What would you think of someone who talked while *you* performed?' And, giving me that smile — with his mouthful of white teeth which were not then exclusively false — he said, 'Ah, but you see, when *I* perform, no one talks.' 'Then,' said I, 'the difference is that *your* audience is composed only of civilised persons.' "

Gianni sang as he drove us to Herculaneum in his new car. He could sing arias, and knew Neapolitan songs by the dozens — "Libero Bovio, Salvatore di Giacomo, those are the names to learn at Naples. Never mind about King Ladislas, or Joachim Murat." When we approached the royal palace at Portici he slowed down. "Look at this. Who but a Neapolitan would have a country retreat with the road going right through the house? And at the foot of an active volcano." He laughed, and thumped his hand on the wheel, highly satisfied with the folly of the Bourbons.

Gianni was something of a patriot. That is to say that all foreigners, and particularly Anglo-Saxons, came in for a mauling. "The names these people have," he remarked, although my name was practically the same as his. "Where do they get them from. I had an actress once — I mean, in a film I directed — a skinny-looking thing like you, English, called Sally. Imagine, *salt*. A fine name for a girl."

I leant forward, my elbows along the back of their seat, my chin bumping on my enlaced knuckles. The nape of Gioconda's neck, rising out of a crimson coat, was whiter than her throat, as if in summer her hair had hung down over it; above this whiteness, twisted glossy ropes of hair were secured by a comb of curved tortoiseshell.

"Your comb. I never saw anything like it."

Her fingers came up to touch it. "How old is it, do you think? Or an old copy of something old? Here — and here — there must have been stones; diamonds, even, for the rest of the work is so fine. I found it on a barrow in San Biagio — one of those barrows, you must have seen them, where they sell, or try to sell, cracked saucers and broken keyrings, rubbish scavenged from here and there.

I took it home and cleaned it. And Gianni liked it." Here Gianni gave a possessive, endorsing nod. "I've worn it for years."

It was a pale, cold day, quiet as a weekday. We were almost alone on the road. At Resina, with the Vesuvius rising over us, we came into a country market where a dozen stunted donkeys, each dragging its own teetering Vesuvius of ill-corded bales, applied their muzzles humidly to the Maserati as it inched among them. Not long afterwards this little town founded on the lava was submerged under the eruption of skyscrapers flung up by a housing project.

At Herculaneum we were the only visitors, wandering unaccompanied through vacant Roman rooms, like guests who have arrived on the wrong day and can take stock of things without having to be polite. Gianni loved my pleasure in the ruins, proud as if the town were his own creation, explaining the arrangement of the houses, the changes of situation caused by volcanic action — "Here was the sea, then, with gardens and cypress alleys leading down to it. All that land down there came much later." Every so often he would tell us, "It was a marvellous life," as if he himself had been plucked out of it.

"Look at this, for instance." Gianni led me away to the foot of one of the corridor-like streets and into an ornate room that had served, possibly, as a private theatre — one end giving a sense of proscenium, decorated with a stone mask set above mosaics of animals and garlands. "What could be more charming." He followed me up the room to examine the decorations and, taking me by the shoulders, stood me in the niche intended for some statue. He then kissed me — or attempted to, his mouth roughly glancing over my chin and throat as I spun my head away, dodging his caress like a blow. He dropped his hands from my shoulders but still stood blocking the way, looking at me and smiling, and repeating in a normal voice, "What could be more charming."

I stood in the niche where he had placed me. Even to push him away seemed too much like a response. In an undertone he complained to me, "Why the fuss. I am only, so to speak, observing the conventions."

"Damn you," I said in English, furious that Gioconda's proximity somewhere in this labyrinth obliged me to lower my voice to him like an accomplice. "Damn you and your conventions."

Gianni walked away. Having stepped down through the narrow doorway he turned back, one hand raised and resting on the outer wall, to look at me with the same bright eyes and hard, humorous compression of the lips.

"Just one moment," said Gioconda, out of sight. Gianni stood quite still. In the street beyond there was a tiny sound, and Gioconda appeared beside him winding her camera. "It was so natural," she said. "So like you."

Gioconda later gave me this photograph, along with one or two others she took that day. I have it still, and there is Gianni, smiling ironically out of the picture at something that has momentarily taken his fancy.

I remained some minutes more in that small Roman theatre — that had, I daresay, seen a lot of this kind of thing played out in various costumes.

Gianni made, I thought, a reference to this incident, in the car as we drove on around the gulf to Sorrento — observing to Gioconda that he found me young for my age. "Strange to think," he said, as if I were not present, "that there are only six or seven years between you two. You seem like my contemporary, while she —" tipping his head back in my direction — "might just be leaving school. Or entering it."

Over his shoulder he gave me, too — again as if the matter were crucial and personal to him — accounts of the great eruption, quoting Pliny to us as though to back up his own testimony, citing like fresh evidence the letters of the poet Statius. "You see how it is with us," he said — meaning Italians, or perhaps the human race. "The ships were waiting to take them off. Ash and lava were streaming down on them. But they had dinner, they talked, they went to the baths, they slept. And then it was too late."

I could see that he thought well of them for this, just as he had commended the impracticality of the Bourbons; and quite expected him to add, as he did, "There is something to be said for it, after all." And when I, still sulking, made no reply, he most unfairly shrugged at Gioconda as if to give me up as a bad job.

Of that journey, with Vesuvius slowly turning us on its

flank, then releasing us for the long arc of the bay, there remains a childhood sensation of disappointment: my outing had been spoilt, the expedition had shifted character in an unlooked-for way. In memory there is a blur of cold sea and silver fields, and then we are at Sorrento and I am cheerful again, having had my lunch and being excited by the pretty restaurant, the romance of the slopes above and cliffs below, and the great view out to Capri. It is as Gianni has just said, I am as easily diverted as a schoolgirl.

The restaurant supplied the usual pair of musicians, small elderly wielders of accordion and fiddle, one of whom — the one with the wall eye — sang in a voice reedily tender, shaken with infirmity. There was also a fortune-teller, who had little to do in the winter months when the clientele were off seeking their fortunes by other means. She fell on us the moment we entered. Gianni purchased our freedom with a few coins, and we watched her go to work — her gypsy costume topped by a worn grey cardigan — on the only other patrons of the restaurant, a ravishing blonde girl and her white-haired escort, who interrupted the process with bursts of delighted laughter in which the fortune-teller joined herself from time to time, the gold hoops in her ears bouncing joyfully on the neck of her cardigan.

"That's the kind of future to have," Gioconda said to us. "It's got them laughing already, just the idea of it."

"It's not difficult to imagine what she's telling them."

Gianni drew his fingers lightly along Gioconda's arm resting on the tablecloth.

Gioconda and I watched the other table. The affair grew more serious, the couple drawing together as they listened, sometimes glancing at one another and half-smiling to assure themselves that it was fantasy.

Gianni was bored. "It's utterly transparent. They pick out a few things that happen to everybody, and make a revelation of it."

"Psychologists too," Gioconda agreed, "will often explain the most obvious things to you as if they were professional discoveries. What's alluring is the illusion, not even of power, but of authority. Isn't that what we want, from gods, priests, poets, even from those columns in the newspaper that answer letters? The possibility that someone really knows, and has got the upper hand of it all."

I said, "Some people do know more than others. That contributes to the impression that someone, somewhere, knows the whole thing."

"Neapolitans know a lot," said Gianni. "But they know it collectively. Break them up, take them away, and they're hopeless, just as stupid as anyone else. It's the city, the phenomenon of Naples itself, that knows something. It's like an important picture, or a book — once you've taken it in, you can't believe there was a time when you didn't know it." He turned to me. "This will change everything for you, being here. Naples is a leap. It's through the looking-glass." And I looked out at the oval mirror of the bay.

There was no more laughter from our companions. In the end their fortunes proved sobering. They parted from the seer in low voices, and a few more coins changed hands. When they got up to go, the man put his arm around the girl, and drew her to him and kissed her cheek — in consolation, perhaps, or with a premonition of loss.

Shortly after these meetings with Gioconda, I moved out of the hotel and took an apartment on the sea, along the foot of the Posillipo. In the sea, one might have said, since the apartment was in one of the villas that stand out in the bay all along the northern arc of Naples, and have a water life of their own. Beginning at Mergellina with a crumbling seventeenth-century colossus, they end at Gaiola with a Roman ruin; their names alone are an inventory of the eccentric. These buildings look on to the gulf of Naples, and are interspersed with grottoes and declivities of the pale gold stone of which that shore is composed, and even with shreds of a disappearing countryside and surviving groups of umbrella pines. Above them rises the headland of the Posillipo — already then encumbered with a ridge or two of the modern blocks that were to deface it completely over the next few years.

An open-air nightclub, wedged into the tufa near my building, lay in wait for its season; and a bedraggled restaurant or two commanded, from scruffy terraces, the incomparable, lake-like prospect of the bay.

In order to reach the apartment one entered quite a
different building, that stood higher on the hillside, above
and behind. From this one went down, in a tiny bathy-
sphere of an elevator, through rock, and arrived at one
end of a long corridor roughly tunnelled from solid
stone, painted and tiled dark red. The corridor could be
lit by a series of electric buttons whose sequence, timed
for a loping run, provided a certain claustrophobic excitement. This deep crossing passed under Via Posillipo
and through the tiny promontory of which my villa
formed the prow. It ended in a flight of steep steps and a
grilled door, beyond which were light, sky, and the sea.
A glassed-in catwalk had been attached to the villa's side,
leading past the doors of the many apartments into which
the house had been divided.

Nothing could have been more canny, more uncanny,
more Neapolitan, than this means of access. "Romantic,"
I wrote of it to Norah — and it did have something of the
sinister that is an authentic element of romance.

There was another approach, by water, disembarking
at a landing stage of stone steps glossy with moss, being
admitted to the house through another green-grilled
door. The building itself was red stucco, lifted clear of
the water on foundations of grey stone; seen from a distance it floated forward in air like a rusty boat in the
slips.

I had two big rooms there, and they were the most
beautiful rooms, by far, that I had lived in. Like most

missionaries, we lived better than those we had come to save; immunities and allowances broke our fall into this new ambience, we had cars to drive us and maids to keep us clean. My rooms gave on to a narrow terrace that, in turn, looked directly across the sea to the volcano: the rooms, the terrace, were like antechambers to the spectacle, their purpose was to disclose it. That view of the Bay of Naples has passed the point where it can ever find its master, its Guardi or its Canaletto; has become virtually a comic sight in art, its configurations too intimately known, even to those who have never seen them, now to be revealed. It gives an impression of indifference to the role humanly assigned to it — as if it will go on lending itself to posters, to chocolate boxes, without ever giving itself away; just as Vesuvius goes on absorbing the tributes of those it clearly intends to exterminate.

There was another floor of apartments, then the water. One might have fished from the terrace. At the rear, where the apartment was entered from the glass walk, there was a wide hallway, and an inner room lined with immense wardrobes and camphor-saturated chests. The whole place was densely, darkly furnished, with great bed and mighty chairs, long table, carved sofa; a flimsier note occasionally struck, like the triangle in an orchestra, by a black tripod plant stand from UPIM or a gilt magazine holder, like an outsize toastrack, from the Rinascente. In the kitchen, small stove and smaller sink flanked a huge old splay-footed refrigerator; while beneath this triptych were predellas of endless cabinets and drawers containing here a cheese-grater, there a corroded colander, or a corkscrew still impaling its wine-dark cork. On the bathtub, an imported fitting hailed you in your own language: WASTE.

Of the heavy dark chests and chairs, several were subsequently stacked in a box-room beyond the kitchen, while others were dragged away at my request and made their way into various unprotesting flats in the building. There was a long stairway like a stone ladder, without turns or landings, leading from the sea right up to the road, and any object too large for the elevator was heaved up or down this cliffway. So that one might at any time observe a packing case or a bureau coming painfully down on somebody's hooped back; and once, looking from the kitchen window, I saw a great rubber tree in a pot, moving in this way, among the pines, to Dunsinane.

Gianni and Gioconda came to see my flat one evening, bringing with them a tub of narcissus. Since Gianni had never been known to carry anything, the pot was held by a small boy who arrived behind them with his face buried in the suffocating flowers. To my surprise Gianni praised everything — he was delighted with the house and with the strangeness of the approach to it. "You're beginning to get the idea," he said, as if I had shown myself an apt pupil.

It was a freezing night: Gianni tried to light the single

fireplace, but the flue would not draw and we sat in our coats in front of a tiny electric stove that scorched the tiles, and our feet, and was otherwise heatless. They drank to my new life in whisky I had obtained that day, duty-free, from the PX.

The sight of this unmanned, woman's enterprise moved Gianni at once to take command. "You could have the chimney altered to make it work," he said. "But that takes brains. In Rome it might be worth doing, even though it's not your own place, but here . . . When it comes to building, Neapolitans have good ideas about form and colour, and there it stops. They can't hang a picture without knocking the wall down."

After they had gone I put the lamps out and looked through the flawed, icy glass of the terrace doors at the lighted city to the left. Behind my back the radiator put out its ineffectual red tonguetips. The window returned my breath, slightly steamy with PX whisky and merged with the smell of narcissus and of the charred fire that Gianni could not light. It was in this confusion of the ignominious and grandiose that I experienced the first moments of pure happiness.

## ❧ V ❧

THE MISSION I had accompanied from England was composed, for the most part, of military men. When I joined it I knew nothing of the professional soldier in modern times. Seething is the word I find for them: many of those people, particularly the officers, were perpetually seething — with fury, with fear, and with the daily necessity of striking out before they could be felled by inapprehensible foes. Of this seething, their profession was but the logical extension. (In fact, their attitude to their authorised enemies — Soviets, socialists, and agitators of all breeds — was tinged with a wistful worship: "Catch *them* putting up with a mess like this" or "*They* wouldn't tolerate this set-up for a second.") My London life, deficient as it had been, had not included those who perceived solutions in the violent deaths of numberless others, and who passionately advocated this view.

Their cruelty could not be shamed. No revelation of its origins or its consequences abashed them. Armoured with the most brutal of emotions, self-pity, they were in-vulnerable to the human claims of others.

These days I would be more comprehending of them, and less tolerant; but then I was baffled by all the seething and tried, quite mistakenly, to make allowances for it. I should never have got mixed up with them. But on the whole, having the compensations of the city, was more contented than any of them; and vaguely suspect for being so.

I had fallen to the lot of the English colonel in whose office I sat. A great seether, he had been military attaché at any number of British embassies, whose superior organization he often cited to us. He was small and trim, with a thin mouth beneath a thin bristle of moustache, shiny little shoes, and an upright bearing; taken together, these attributes conveyed a state of continual defiance. As a child he must have been impressed with the merit of looking people in the eyes, and had in consequence developed a fixed glare that so revealed him that, out of common humanity, one could only look away. He had been divorced, and lived alone on the Posillipo, in a building next to mine. It was arranged that the car that called for him each morning should bring me, too, to our offices at Bagnoli, and in this way I started the day with him a full half-hour earlier than might otherwise have been the case.

One morning, as we stood side by side in wintry sunshine, he and I, waiting for the car to change the setting of our silence, J. P. Tulloch drew up to the curb in a dark green M.G.

He threw the door open for me. "I'm going to Bagnoli. Hop in." When I was in and had closed the door, he waved to the Colonel — whom he did not know — made a U-turn, and we set off down the hill towards Mergellina.

*"So light to the croupe the fair lady he swung,*

*So light to the saddle before her he sprung,"* he recited, sing-song.

I said, "I hope he doesn't mind. The Colonel."

"How can he mind? There are only two seats — and he would hardly expect me to take him instead. How can he mind?"

"You'd be surprised how he can mind." I was pleased with the turn my morning was taking, riding along in the sharp air without the Colonel. The man was breezy too — I had not seen him since the day of first meeting Gioconda, when his manner had been, as I described it to her, tightly furled.

"Much has been said and written about the military mind. Nothing, however, harsh enough."

"They're appalling," I agreed. Then went on, mealy-mouthed, "I suppose one ought to be more tolerant."

"Why, pray? I am a man, and everything inhuman is alien to me. All right, giggle away then. What's he doing there, straddling your doorstep?"

I wondered how he knew about my doorstep. I explained how we lived, the Colonel and I, side by side. "He's divorced," I said.

"So am I," said Justin Tulloch.

"Well . . . you'll marry again."

"But will it be any different?"

He was more of an oddity than I'd imagined, telling me these serious things in a kind of banter that made it difficult to know how to take them. I had a sense, not agreeable, of being deliberately put at a disadvantage. I twisted round in the seat. "He's right behind us. The Colonel."

The M.G. went faster.

" *'She is won! we are gone, over bank, bush, and*
*scaur;*

*They'll have fleet steeds that follow,' quoth young*
*Lochinvar.*

I hope that's your favourite poem," he said, "as it is mine, and that of every thinking person."

"I don't like the part where he says about there being better-looking women who'd be glad to marry him."

" *'There are maidens in Scotland more lovely by far*
*Who would gladly be bride to the young Lochinvar.'*
Well, it was only a ruse."

"The sort of ruse," I said, "that one wouldn't be likely to forget."

"True love," said Justin Tulloch, "is the cultivation of forgetfulness. And don't you forget it. In any case, I won't hear anything against Lochinvar. Listen to this:

'*The bride kissed the goblet, the knight took it up,*
  *He quaffed off the wine, and threw down the cup —*'
No, I'll not hear a word against it. As a Scottish Nationalist, which I happen to be." I said nothing, and he went
on, "You don't believe it, but I am."

"I do believe it." In fact it seemed very likely he
might follow some unexpected cause of the kind. I fancied he was disappointed that I showed no surprise.
"Have you moved from the hotel? How did you happen
to come past at this hour?" Then it occurred to me that it
was indiscreet to ask him this.

"I expect to be in that hotel for months. I've been at
my Italian lesson, and was going — am going — to
Nisida, about my lawful business." On the enisled cape
of Nisida, off Bagnoli, there were other offices, other
officials. He said, "Write down your telephone number
for me." After a silence he continued, "All right: please
write down your telephone number, I implore you to
write down your telephone number."

"I don't have a pencil and paper."

He took his left hand off the wheel and reached in his
pocket. "There. As a matter of fact I tried to get it from
your office, but they wouldn't give it out. Possibly your
po-faced Colonel wants to keep you for himself. I did get
your address." He took the paper back from me. "What
do you do in the evenings? Do you have friends here?"

I told him about Gioconda, and how I had met them
both on the same day.

Justin often drove me to work after that, and we began
to see one another now and then in the evenings. There
was a studied irregularity to our meetings, and if at any
of them we particularly enjoyed each other's company he
would then stay away for a week, or two, or three, it was
part of his neurosis of self-protection. I think that his
anxiety to remain uncommitted had been aroused, so far
as I was concerned, at the very moment of his taking an
interest in me, the one operating in conjunction with the
other; and made it impossible for him to be natural. The
reserved, unaffected person with whom I had worked that
December morning at the Hotel Royal was never again
revealed to me: the more I was to know Justin, the
further we were to get from his spontaneous, direct self,
and the more enmeshed in badinage and circumlocution.
Even his appearance was altered somewhat by dissimu-
lation.

I minded this only moderately. What I minded most
was its being manifest and yet unmentionable. I was not
as ready as his caution suggested to offer him, or anyone,
the devotions of love: for that, I was at least as unready
as he. The offence to my vanity in his casual exploitation
of my company would, so I coolly felt, be avenged the
first time he attempted to make love to me. Meantime I
rather enjoyed his erratic companionship. I enjoyed
something else, too — the new sensations of power and
control that went with what I have just said; the knowledge that I had ceased to be accommodating. I suppose

this is what is known as the loss of innocence. I had no cause to regret my lost innocence, for it had never done me any good: I have lived a much more virtuous life without it.

It was extraordinary, though, the way Justin's defensive, flippant tone imposed itself. One would find oneself falling into line, making elaborately absurd under- or overstatements to meet the mocking tone he set, using antiquated schoolgirl phrases to amuse him, describing a colleague as "a juggins," saying "ripping" or "spiffing" or "jolly-dee." Even to die was to "keel over," just as to live was to "press on regardless." This ironic jargon became the bond between us; we operated, the two of us, in code.

Cosy private jokes of language, used against themselves, were the sort of thing that, in leaving England, I had wished to escape from. Yet their resuscitation in that bizarre setting gave them a nostalgic — almost an anthropological — interest. That is something one does not foresee in wishing to elude one's traditions: that the threat, once its fangs are drawn, may become transfigured into intimacy, a frame of reference. In the same way that the forms of social class, or of an oppressive religion, are retrospectively regarded with sentimental longing when — and simply because — their influence has been extinguished.

Justin, when alone with me, talked quite a lot, often incorporating an instructive note into his whimsical speeches. If he wished to terminate a conversation, he would wait till I began to deliver my own views and then cut me off in mid-sentence: it was one of his man-made defences, part of his plan of attack. Irritated at the beginning, I later would lead him on in order to observe his technique. One day he noticed, I think, from my smile that this was so, for he turned my face to his and said, "To grow older and bolder, Jenny: those are things to be shunned." And when I did not answer, he urged me, "Don't turn into a cool customer, Jenny. I don't like it."

I told him, "When I was a warm customer, I was asked to cool off."

His greatest compliment was that I was "old-fashioned." "There you go again," he would say, but approvingly, of some judgment of mine, some turn of phrase. "What an old-fashioned girl you are, Jenny." This was, I suppose, a tribute to the lost innocence; but I looked on that, with my interesting new detachment, as something of which I still possessed merely the physical attributes — as at school, when I noticed that teachers found me particularly attentive and would sometimes address themselves exclusively to me, though my thoughts were all the time elsewhere: it must have been some accident of expression, or the unblinking nature of my adolescent stare. So with that impression of an obliging openness that Justin valued in me. I believed it to be no more than a habit I was beginning to grow out of. It would take time — a lifetime perhaps — to lose the outward aspect of an ingenuousness I no longer completely possessed. It was a deception I did not seek, but which I did nothing to dispel.

My new awareness had not extended, as yet, to finding in all this anything to mourn, on his side or on mine.

There was a larger reason for not minding this casual courtship of Justin's, and that was the city itself. In our office, in those days, I was always aware of the city, like someone compelled at a dinner table to be attentive to a boring neighbour while listening all the time for the voice of a loved one at the other end of the room. Since I was willing to do any errand that took me into town, they sent me out every so often in the back of the Vehicle to buy cameos or corals for visiting generals, or to get opera tickets for an association of military wives who called themselves the Culture Vultures.

By these means I was able to meet Gioconda occasionally in the centre of town. Standing up at a counter we would have coffee, fierce black coffee, a spoonful apiece, served in tiny cold cups that were always wet from the draining board. Or she would take me, on some general's behalf, to a source of table-cloths, or gloves, or tortoise-shell boxes. We made an expedition of the kind one bitter day towards the end of that year, when the Colonel sent me out to find him a genuine Christmas tree to replace the miniature nylon one that had been issued to him. I don't suppose the Colonel's commission was as hilarious as it appeared to us, but I remember that Gioconda and I went together to Via Foria, where the trees were sold, giggling all the way like schoolgirls and wiping away tears of joy. The slain trees, niggard and meridional, lay about in dismal heaps in a little park there, and we walked round in the cold examining them. A merchant heating his hands over an improvised brazier was astounded by our request for a better specimen, flinging his hands apart then quickly re-aligning them over the coals. He reminded us this was not Canada and advised me to take what was going — which I did, lugging it back to Bagnoli in the Vehicle.

I had not had a female friend since childhood, and novelty made this one the more singular. Perhaps it was something the same for her. At her house, from time to time, I was to meet women she had gone to school with, a relative who lived at Vico Equense, two plump girls, twin sisters, with a curious English name that derived from the Napoleonic wars. She might recount to me a conversation she had had at some dinner party or on the telephone, but the very diversity of these connections suggested that she had no single close friend — no friend, in fact, closer than I.

For my part, I kept Gioconda to myself, as I had in writing to Norah. I had no circle to which I might have admitted her. I could have introduced her to Justin, but I feared his comments on Gianni — whom he quickly characterised, from my accounts, as a blatherskite. In the same way, Gianni would refer to this unknown acquaintance of mine as *"lo Scozzese,"* as if a Scotsman were scarcely entitled to a name of his own. For Gianni, who was always urging me to extend my experience, resented even so mild a show of interest in any man other than himself.

Gioconda's English was excellent, though she had little use of it in Naples. Gianni spoke English poorly and rarely, though priding himself on idiomatic phrases that he always got wrong — the crucial word getting omitted or mispronounced — and which he would preface accusingly with "as they put it in England," or "as the English say." (Gioconda, on the contrary, would occasionally make over-literal renderings into English, saying "belfry" for *campanile*, or "Saint Januarius" for San Gennaro; and once, preposterously, speaking of "the Carabineers.") They both spoke good French, and once in a while, curiously, they spoke it to one another. I suppose they wished sometimes to escape from the succession of trenchant ironies that are the conversational fate of cultivated Italians, but I noticed that this usually happened when they were in some way agitated — Gioconda, who detested the telephone, would call out, *"Sois un ange, prends le téléphone"* if she heard the bell from an adjoining room; or Gianni, berating her for some imagined shortcoming, would cry, *"Mais tu es bête,"* reserving for tenderer moments his Italian endearment, *"Cretina."*

There are things one will not say in one's own language, they carry too much weight; to have said them in another tongue is an extenuating circumstance, like being drunk or demented. So Justin, too, if he admired the style of my hair or the colour of my shawl, would be foolishly italianate, crying *"Bellissima"* or *"Un amore"*; or might even comment, quite soberly, *"Che bel colore."*

Entering Gioconda's flat late one Friday, I passed from room to room without finding her, at last hearing voices from the terrace. It was January and the days were then as fine as spring, but that was the first night mild enough to sit outside. The sight of the doors open to the evening expanded the terse, wintry sense of darkness instantly, luxuriously, into summer. On the threshold I heard their voices more clearly — but low, insistent, and speaking French. They were leaning on the balustrade with their backs to me, side by side but not, it was clear, together. Gioconda's head was the lower; Gianni's was slightly turned to her as he talked. I could tell that they were quarrelling. And I realised that Gianni was asking something of Gioconda, and she was refusing him.

It was dismaying to come upon them like that. A loss of equilibrium, frightening, like overhearing one's parents quarrel. For I had come to rely on them, even then, to provide me with a measure of stability. Of course Gianni gave Gioconda a hundred reasons a day to quarrel with him, but the fact was that she never accepted the provocation, her love apparently directed to some idea of Gianni — some misconception as I saw it — more profound, more entire, that allowed her to overlook his irascibility as no more than a bad habit. I had got used to this imbalance, this counterpoise of their relations, and was beginning to depend on it as something immutable.

More distressing still was the glimpse of Gianni as ✓ supplicant. As long as he had continued to antagonise me with his dictatorial ways, I had been required to consider him in no other light. Besides, there had been an infuriating consistency to him. Now I felt I might have to take account of something more, even to feel humiliated for him as one would not have felt for someone less committed to self-assertion.

*"Ne dis pas non,"* he said to her, and put the flat of his hands together on the wide stone railing. *"Penses-y un peu."*

Gioconda shook her head. I heard few words of what she said. *". . . déjà . . . pourrait pas durer."* She trailed her forefinger along the convex railing in a preoccupied yet conclusive gesture; as she might have drawn it down the keyboard of a piano before closing the lid.

Tosca, quietly letting me out, said merely, *"Ah Signorina mia"* — whether addressing me, or speaking of Gioconda, one could not know.

[ 69 ]

# ❧ VI ❧

Having cleared my rooms, I started to add to them small objects of my own. Most Saturday afternoons were free now, and I would take a bus across the city to the junkstalls (the "junkies," as Gianni in his English called them) in Piazza Francese, or to antique shops in Via Costantinópoli, to buy a little painting on glass, or a shelf of flowers painted on gesso, or a piece of fissured majolica. Afterwards I might walk down into San Biagio dei Librai and spend an hour or two with Gioconda before taking these purchases home. On weekends Gianni was often there — usually dismissing my jugs and plates as rubbish; at other times approving them but ridiculing the price which, according to him, no Italian would have dreamt of paying.

"You might as well go to the swellies in Via Chiatamone," he would cry, saying "swellies" in English and mispronouncing the name of the street to make an obscene pun, an allusion to the prostitutes who patrolled it in the evening. "If you go to the junkies, you should pay the junky price." I could hardly conceive of paying less than I did — for the prices of these meaner fragments of the eighteenth century had not then begun to climb — and throughout that winter continued to visit the *rigattieri*, letting Gianni rave on about my gullibility. It was strange how one did let him rave on: one found oneself letting his complaints pass uncontested, just as Gioconda did. He had a knack of eliciting indulgence — or perhaps it was merely that Gioconda's indulgence of him was contagious. One was always letting him off with something — with his fault-finding, his bragging, his ludicrous English — quite as if, in return, he were making some immeasurable, compensating addition to our lives.

One weekend of that New Year I came into Gioconda's hallway carrying my Castelli saucer, or jug of Montelupo wrapped in newspaper. The weather had turned cold again and I had walked down slippery streets through a bleak drizzle. Gioconda had a fire in her little room, and a streaked saucepan of coffee stood on the tiles in front of it. She had on an old polo-necked pullover blotched with paint; her hair was uncombed, and she kept lifting wisps of it out of the neck of the sweater with her forefinger.

"Gianni isn't coming this weekend," she told me. "He has a big wheel there from America." She briefly described this *pezzo grosso*, whom she had met once or twice when she travelled with Gianni to California — "sentimental, efficient, a cultured man who makes an affectation of crassness."

I said, "To think of you in America."

"I liked it," she said. "Though less than Gianni did."

"Gianni's always saying he hated it."

"Well . . . you know." Gioconda obviously considered it a lapse of taste on my part, this holding of Gianni to his words. She said, "I liked the monuments." I thought she must mean the sights, the landmarks — redwoods, Chrysler Building — but she went on, "The statues, I mean, of the national heroes. In Italy they're usually riding chargers and brandishing swords. There, they are often in armchairs."

I thought this outrageous from a woman who had given herself to a man of action.

She lifted her chin towards the window, indicating her own street. "In New York the buildings are silver, or white, or yellow, so smooth, so glossy, as if they were made of wax."

"All the same, I don't see you living there."

"I don't see myself living anywhere but here. That's it — what we quarrel about," she added, acknowledging my presence on that previous evening. "It's too late for me to live in those countries, away from the discomforts of home . . . But I like the humour, the common sense. And there are so many harmless people: Italians are seldom harmless. And when they are at ease, those northern people, it means more than it does with us, it's so pleasant that one wants to encourage them, to say, 'Smile, be natural' — the way one does taking a photograph, urging as natural the rarest expression of all."

She fingered a loose stitch of her sleeve, drawing it out until it started to shred. "Gianni wants me to live in Rome." Now she began to work the thread back into its place. "It's logical," she went on, as usual defending Gianni's point of view. "If we could be married, for instance, it would be automatic, wouldn't it?"

"And since you can't be married, this is what you have. Being here is all you have."

"There you are." She raised her eyes to mine. She smiled. "One stays here out of self-preservation."

She had expressed it precisely, for only by some extreme instinct of self-defence could she have resisted the natural wish for a common life with her lover. Apparent in their conversation — in the simplest enquiry, "Do you take mushrooms?" or "Are these your gloves?" — was the lack of a shared domestic life that all their greater intimacy could not replace.

"And yet," she said, "who would not wish, at times, to leave this place of poverty, to live where a street is not a corridor of want and filth and suffering? Of course I would like to change, to get away: I too."

"You would miss it, then."

"Yes. But that's a way to go on loving — a place, or a person. To miss it. In fact, to go away, to put yourself in the state of missing, is sometimes the simplest way to preserve love."

"It seems to me something that Gianni would understand, your staying here."

"He does understand it."

"Then why does he make a quarrel of it?"

Gioconda looked at me. "You see, *I* am the one who quarrels. Because in Rome there are other women . . . There are other women . . . And he says that would stop if I came to Rome and lived with him." She went on at once, to check her own distress, "Let's have our coffee."

I brought over the tray that stood on her desk, and she poured coffee from the battered saucepan. The cups were veined, like my finds in Via Costantinópoli, but heavy with Victorian roses. Along Gioconda's cheek, as she leant to fill them, a single escaped hair lay, itself like a fine fracture in porcelain.

"Luciana — my sister — lives at Nice in one of those flats, a glassed-in crow's nest, that were the latest thing in the Thirties, modern by my standards, with heating and faultless plumbing, and a machine that does the washing . . . Her son attends the *lycée*, she has the day to herself. In the morning, walks to the esplanade, reads the paper in the café; stops in, on the way home, at a lending library behind the Hotel Ruhl. In the afternoon, plays cards with a friend; in the evening, watches television. Incredible as it may seem, none of this causes her to miss Naples. When she comes here, one sight of San Biagio is enough to have her longing for the shiny shop fronts of Nice, one day in this house has her yearning after her well-fitting windows and fuses that do not blow.

Growing up here, and the war, have been too much for her. Just being comfortable will keep her contented for the rest of her life."

After a moment she said, "That's all wrong. I make it sound like nothing." She sighed as though remonstrating with, as though patiently correcting, someone other than herself. She handed me my cup, and held the pot poised above her own. "Luciana's husband belonged to a Resistance group that was formed in 1940, at the fall of France. They called themselves *Les Quarantes*. In '43 he was taken by the Germans. She went to the prisons, trying to find where he was, if he was alive, if he was still in France. She did find him, at the prison in the Boulevard Raspail. They wouldn't let her see him, but she could take his washing and bring it back. She opened the seam of a shirt and put in the lead of a pencil and a slip of paper. The paper came back to her in another shirt: he had written on it, simply, *'J'ai faim'* . . . One day she went there bringing back his washing, and the guards laughed and told her, 'He won't need those any more.' She fainted away on the floor, and they put her in the street."

She said, "Forgive me, it's terrible. But I made it sound trivial before — the way she lives, and why. Sometimes it seems easier to cheapen things than remember them."

We were quiet. She poured her coffee, exactly as though the gesture had been arrested while she spoke and might now continue. I held my cup in both hands and sat back on the divan with my legs beneath me. I looked up at the opposite wall. "Gioconda," I asked her, "who painted those white flowers?"

Gioconda stared up at the picture as if she sought the information from it. She sat back on the divan alongside me, and let the cat climb on to her knees. She drank, and each time she lowered her cup the cat peered short-sightedly into it.

"My father," she said, "was walking in a street in Rome, centuries ago, long before the war. And he saw that painting through a doorway, it was inside a gallery. At first he thought it might be by De Pisis, but as he looked at it through the open door he could see it was not, and he went in to ask who the artist was. The dealer told him it was a young painter, very poor, who had a studio in a slum out near Porta Portese. My father wrote to the artist but there was no reply. He then went and called on him."

Gioconda began to stroke the cat, softly, downward, until it purred, as if it were a stringed instrument from which she could draw responses. "He found a young man, twenty-two, solitary as a scarecrow, with the speech of a poor Roman . . . He was entering a new phase of work, he said, and when my father told him he had bought the painting in the shop — this painting — he replied that he wished he had destroyed it. He showed my father some drawings, and a few canvases that were on stretchers against the wall, but he would part with nothing. He had a reason for keeping everything — this was from a series, that was unfinished, and so on. When my father left he seemed glad to see the last of him."

Gioconda tipped her head back against the wall, and went on, slowly strumming the cat. "The following day he came to the hotel where my father was staying and asked him to sell the picture back. My father took him to lunch in a restaurant, where they spent most of that afternoon. The picture was not mentioned again, and soon after that the painter came and spent some weeks here, at Naples. My parents made a studio for him in another part of this house. After a while he disappeared back to Rome, but always came again, turning up without a word, installing himself in the studio, seeing little of the rest of us but once in a while talking with my father all through the night. On the stairs or in the courtyard he would pass us, my sister and me, without a glance. Not proudly, you know, or humbly, but absorbed and apart. He was like a character from Turgenev, without postures, with no sense of role."

"What did he look like?"

She pursed her lips as if trying to remember. "Tall, for an Italian, particularly a poor one. Dark hair, even then receding. Clean-shaven. Dark eyes — dark, that is, and bright at the same time. He wore workman's clothes, anything at all, and in winter a coat he had salvaged off some rubbish dump. Again, there was no pose in it, only poverty; later on, when he began to have money, he ate more, bought himself warm clothes . . . Gradually he became less separate from us, using our names, occasionally letting me run an errand for him — to buy a tube of zinc-white or bring a bundle of rags. He used to borrow my father's books, and that brought him into these rooms. He had two exhibitions, after a while, in Rome; he was written about a bit in magazines. His became a name — not famous, but one of those names that people mention to show they are *à la page;* that sort of thing, that world, was not so obvious then as it is now, at least to us, but he knew what it was and he kept clear of it. With those people, even one's indifference to them has cachet; for them, integrity itself must be a pose.

"Eventually he was able to buy part of a fisherman's house, south of Rome, at the tip of a long peninsula, and he went there to live. He still came here once in a while, and my father occasionally went to see him, sometimes taking me along. Now they are building a road to that peninsula, I'm told it's all spoilt. But then we could only go with difficulty, doing the last part of the journey by foot or on a donkey, or hiring a boat and going round the coast. You wouldn't believe how wild it was — isolated, beautiful. A warren of white houses, the sea in front, the hills behind, on either side a long empty shore of white sand, cactus, rocks, and Roman ruins.

"My father and he were friends, in an outdated, an antiquated sense. They had a friendship of the kind men can no longer have. It would be too simple to introduce complexities, to say he was the son my father did not have, or the artist my father could not be, or to dwell in other ways on his attraction for my father. When I try to describe now, to you, their affection for each other, the only phrase I find is brotherly love."

She had ceased to accompany herself on the cat, which gathered itself up with its paws together on her kneecap, sprang down with a delicate thud, and stalked to the fire. Gioconda picked a few white hairs off her lap, lit a cigarette, and sat up cross-legged on the sofa, balancing her elbow on her knee and her cheek on her left hand.

"He lived there at the sea in four great rooms like caverns, with rough, whitewashed walls, domed roof, stone floor. With no comforts, with luxuries of silence and time. The rooms were damp, bad for the pictures — and for him, since he had a history of tuberculosis. He had a stove in one room, and high up round the wall a sort of wooden gallery where the canvases were stacked. A worktable, a bed, a lamp, a chair."

Gioconda bent forward to shake her cigarette in an ashtray. "It came to me that my father would like us to marry. That is, he hoped I would fall in love. He encouraged it — not crudely, but in ways that were evident to me, young as I was, sixteen, and therefore thinking only of such things — and I resented it. It put me off, as it must, always, as a matter of course. I wouldn't go with my father any more on those excursions that he made."

"And did he, the painter, did he care about you?"

"Those things aren't orderly, or precipitate, like stories. It all took time, too much time, to come about and then to reveal itself. I still saw him when he visited us, but I was distant with him. Ridiculous, I daresay."

How had she looked, that Gioconda of fifteen years before — a reserved girl with a dark, tender beauty, fatter or thinner than now, pensive or gay? Looking at her, hunched forward at my side with the cigarette between her fingers, I dressed her in the fashion of the period, spreading her hair in wide little curls about her shoulders, squaring her sleeves and bodice, trying to divest her face and person of the impressions that had made it adult.

"Mussolini had declared war in the spring of 1940. My father was dismissed from the university. Having detested the regime for years, he now became obsessed with it, it was his only subject. If we went to the cinema to divert him, there would be a newsreel, my father would be convulsed with rage, calling out in the theatre, *"Cafone! Cafone!"* The sight of me in school uniform — on which I had to wear, like other children, the fascist insignia — made him desperate. You will imagine the result of this. Anything might have happened. He was warned once or twice. Then his property was confiscated and we were sent into exile — one of those domestic exiles that were popular then, a species of detention in a remote part of Italy. What they were doing a century ago in Russia under the Tsars — and are doing still; what Mussolini called going forward . . . We were sent to a village in the Abruzzi, a place where the contorted shapes of mountains and valleys seemed to have been intended as background for the convulsed lives we were living. We had a shanty at one end of the town, and helped on the land. Even such a place as that had its representatives of the secret police."

Gioconda was silent, and then began again almost loudly, as if reverting to a central theme from which she had strayed. "It was before this that they quarrelled, my father and the painter of this picture. Throughout the Thirties, during the time when they had perpetually discussed the prospect of horrors that were now coming to pass, they had conceived themselves, I suppose, to be in agreement. If he had told my father that he was *un obiettore di coscienza* — what's the English expression, opposed to taking arms?"

"Same. Conscientious objector."

"Yes, if he had said that before, as he probably did, many times, then my father had not taken it seriously — at least, he must have believed that when the time came it would be different. When war broke out, he — the painter — was in any case exempt from military service because of having had tuberculosis; at that time there were not these new drugs, of course, and he had never been completely cured. He stayed on at the sea working, perhaps more troubled even than my father by what was taking place. He turned to himself again and became more as he was when we knew him first. Still he visited us while we remained at Naples, and now that was because of me. Are you cold?"

Gioconda got up and added a log to the fire, rasping it into position with jabs of the poker. She dusted her palms together and came back to me. A car started up in the courtyard, failed, and began again.

"My father and he began to disagree. To my father it was indecent, in those circumstances, to shut oneself in a room. Any resistance, organized or futile, seemed better to him than that. To the painter, it was the only course — to stay in one's room and go on painting. He said, 'I *am* in the resistance' . . . Then we were sent to the mountains, and we didn't see him for over a year. Not until my mother's death."

The cat sat up on its haunches, showing its long, tufted underside, and sharpened its claws on an upholstered chair — plucking away as delicately and accurately at each of the upraised threads as if it were now, in its turn, pursuing the musical theme.

"When my mother died, in our shack in the mountains, he somehow got word of it. He had been in Naples and heard of it through Tosca's brother, whom he met in the street. He came to our village there — a fearful journey at that time, what with the war and the winter, and he did most of it on foot." Gioconda lit another cigarette, and over it looked directly at me to divert her mind's eye from what she was describing. "We saw him coming from far off, like a pilgrim — truly like a pilgrim, for the word means one who approaches across the fields . . . We knew it was he. No one else ever walked like that, without the need to make any impression on the world, not even for the worse."

I thought of Gianni — his lordly strut, his straddling stance.

"Of course it was reported. That he came. By then the authorities had more to think about and he got off with a warning, although when he returned to the house at the sea his studio had been torn to pieces. All through that year, while the war was changing, we had no word of him. When it became obvious that Italy would be invaded, my father tried to negotiate secretly, with a bribe, a passage for me through Italy into Switzerland, but that autumn the Germans closed the frontier. They put great nets there, against which the fugitives were caught like birds . . . When the Allied invasion came in the south, everything was confusion, at first we had to stay put. But the bombardment of Naples was unbearable. When we heard Salerno had fallen, we escaped from that village and made the journey, a hideous journey, home."

"How could your father bring you back here — my God, at that moment? Wasn't he afraid?"

"He was afraid of leaving me behind, afraid of what might happen if we stayed. I was older by then and wouldn't have remained without him anyway. When we reached Naples the worst was over — that is to say, the bombardment itself, for every other worst was to come. The city had been through all forms of privation, battered from both sides. Degradation, wretchedness — you won't want to hear it again: for our generation, yours and mine, it is commonplace. Not only what was suffered, but what suffering brought people to. The terrible *details*, that have always been the specialty of Naples, the terrible ironies. While the city was under blackout, you know that the Vesuvius was in eruption, the entire region irradiated with a red glow that could be seen for a hundred miles . . . It was a real hell we were in, bathed in red, overhung by a sky of ash, smelling of fire and brimstone. The mountain was weird, wonderful, the slopes flickering with the sparks thrown up by molten lava. Oh Jenny, while all this was going on, thousands of the poor got into little boats and rowed out to Capri. There was nothing for them there, no way to keep themselves, nothing to eat, they had to come back. It was just an instinct, immemorial, useless, as an animal might step to a mound of higher ground in a tidal wave.

"We lived through it, more easily than most. When the occupation of Rome was completed, the painter came to Naples, came to see us again . . . on a bicycle. He stayed some time, he couldn't get back. My father could not credit he would still keep outside of what was happening. The resistance in Italy had taken on enormous proportions by then. The countryside north of Rome was infiltrated with saboteurs, with soldiers who had deserted the Axis, with escaped Allied prisoners. My father could not believe in any scruple that would exempt a young man from taking part in this. Ultimately — they spoke bitterly to one another, and they parted."

"And you — what did you think?"

"I was young, on those matters I only played at thinking. I had always thought what my parents thought. Now, it seems to me as if time, and other wars, and other wickedness, are on the painter's side. But retrospect is not the same as the event, and that was not like other wars, except in some final, historical perspective; and there is something chilling in a historical perspective consistently applied to daily life.

"So it was," Gioconda went on, apparently in logical continuation of what had gone before, "just at the time when my father never wanted to see this man again, that his original wish was fulfilled and I fell in love. These consequences, these fulfilments, Jenny, these hopes that turn back and terrify you with their consummation. We could hardly ever meet, we couldn't correspond, yet by the end of the war we were lovers."

"And your father?"

"My father came to hate him. For him it was passivity that had allowed Mussolini to have power, and this — premeditated — inaction was inexcusable to him. Perhaps he was right. One cannot live one's own posterity." Her voice accelerated, as if there remained only one item to conclude the story. "I went there, to that place on the sea — I went there to live with him. I broke with my father. We lived there together for a year, just over a year, the whole year of '46." She had made a cradle of her arms crossed on her breast, warming herself. "One day he took a boat, and went to Gaeta. For some errand. It was easiest to go there by boat, as I have said. The boat had a small engine, but half-way there it must have failed."

'Must have' released a thrill of fear in me, like the prospect of physical pain.

"There were oars in the boat. He had to row to shore. He found a sandy place among the rocks where he could land. He pulled the boat up the shore — and on to a mine."

In the early darkness the room was contracting. On the window-ledge a pigeon was winding itself round and round and round like a top.

"Gioconda," said I. "Gioconda."

She lifted her hand from her breast to make a show of her own acceptance; to make her history bearable to *me*.

At last she continued, "I think that killed my father, the war reaching back like that and taking him along with it. I believe it killed my father. It seemed, once more, intended, ordained, after the refusal to engage in it. How it lay in wait for him, that violence, the useless death he had shunned for others and for himself. Another terrible fulfilment. My father came there and took me away. I have never been back. He saw to everything. There were the paintings — some belonged to a dealer, others went to the family — for he still had his family in Rome, his father serving at an *osteria* in Trastevere. Some I kept. My father did everything. We went on, for a dreadful year, together, here in this house. Then he took sick. At first it was said to be an ulcer, but it was cancer, I suppose, from the beginning. In a few months he was dead. The war — in its way, it killed him too."

She said, in another of these asides that were like a drawing of the breath she needed to finish her story, "When I talk of it this way, now, to you, it all comes out as if there were some sequence, some logic, instead of moods, contradictions, alternatives. The design imposes itself afterwards. And is false, must be false.

"Then I wrote that book, you know, *Del Tempo Felice*. During the last months of my father's life. I only knew I must live as long as he was alive. So it was, in a way, as though we both were dying, my time running out along with his. In sleep I would tell myself all that had happened so I wouldn't wake up thinking myself still there — at that place — because remembering happiness was the worst of all, just as the poets say. In suffering, everything is as the poets say . . . Memory was intolerable, I had to set it down, even though that engendered more memories, more and more memories. It was as if I had to get it all done before some great departure. I used to sit by my father's bed at the hospital writing it on my knee, unwilling to stop even when he asked me to read a book or a newspaper to him . . ." Tears at last flowed over her face and she inclined her cheek to her woollen shoulder to rub them off. "I would write it while I ate, while I was falling asleep, while I sat in the bus. It was finished just after my father's death."

She looked at me again. "It was then that Gianni came. And saved my life — as they say." Gioconda, in adding this last phrase, sought to detract from the drama, the melodrama, of what she said enough to allow of its yet being uttered. "What you see — is nothing. No more than a dress of mine is me. He understood entirely . . . entirely. It was a rescue. I had transmitted my message, like a castaway, without hope. Then I was sent for and brought back into the world. He did it all." She repeated, as she had of her father, "He did everything." She said, "He devoted himself to me, to that work of mine. How can one explain? — it did not happen in spite of my loving someone else, it was *because* of my experience that we loved each other."

"Like Othello," I said. "Only the other way round.
'*She loved me for the dangers I had passed,
And I loved her, that she did pity them.*' "

Gioconda got up and crossed the room. She took an envelope out of a drawer of the desk and brought it back to me. There was no trace of her tears at all. She might have been an acquaintance casually showing me the snapshots of some holiday, so expertly had she controlled herself. In the envelope were three photographs of a cadaverous man in a heavy sweater leaning against a chalky wall. There was one picture of Gioconda, the Gioconda of my imaginings, with shoulder-length hair and a tightly belted waist, standing on a beach with her hands behind her back and her bare feet together: it was the stance of a prisoner, but the fresh young face was alight with laughter.

Gioconda replaced the photographs in the envelope, keeping back for an instant the clearest of them and holding it for me to see.

"Gaetano," she said. "His name was Gaetano."

She put the envelope back and closed the drawer. She switched on the lamp that stood on the desk, and we looked at each other anew in the light of her experience. I was convinced she had not spoken like this before, at least not at such length, or dispassionately. Words would have been as presumptuous as an embrace: yet the inadequacy of silence was painful. Trapped in our thoughts and our afterthoughts, we have no impulses left to serve us on such occasions.

She said, "When people say of their tragedies, 'I don't often think of it now,' what they mean is it has entered permanently into their thoughts, and colours everything. Because the idea of Gaetano is always with me, I'm less shocked now, when I suddenly come upon some reminder of him, than I was long ago when he still seemed a grief I must get over. Even a few years back it could still be terrible. In New York, one day, I went into a gallery — one of those dealer's shops with lots of light and carpet. I had really gone in to get warm — it was a freezing day. And on the wall there was a picture of his, painted just after the war. *La Ginestra* — what's that, in English?"

"The gorse. No, the broom."

"I had been buying things — you know, presents from America. I was carrying all the packages in a big paper bag. The girl at the desk kept saying, 'Check your shopping bag. Check your bag, Miss,' and I was staring at his yellow canvas across the room. They had a notice, *Please do not touch the paintings;* they should forbid the paintings to touch *you*." She turned her palm outward to me. "It was nothing unpredictable, was it, after all? But then I felt it like violence done to me. Gianni and I had just become lovers. Oh God, now I've upset this ashtray — it's all right, nothing's alight. It's all gone out by now. Well, I wanted to pay some tribute. I couldn't. leave without — as it were — laying my wreath at this Madison Avenue shrine . . ."

"What, then?"

She smiled. "I asked the price. Such are the gestures of modern love. It was a means of recognition — to have the girl take her eyes off my shopping bag for a moment and consult a list, stumble over Gaetano's name, pronounce '*ginestra*' as if it were a hospital for women's diseases . . . For a moment I made them defer, unknowingly, to my grief, made them take account of our connection. The owner of the gallery even swam out of the wings somewhere, on hearing my question, and came up to me as though I were a bride."

She got to her feet, began to brush at her skirt with both hands. She said, "It's all wrong, what I've told you," as she had said of her sister's story. "But I can come no closer to it."

# ❧ VII ❧

I HAD BEGUN by then to treat the city with a show of familiarity; pretending, as people do with a celebrated acquaintance, to know it better than I did, inserting myself into its landscape, another figure in its vast *presepio*; acquiring habits of cafés and buses and hairdressers, uttering casual observations that sounded on my own ears exotic as examples from a phrase-book: "There is snow on the Apennines" or "Capri is always clearer in bad weather."

The assets of Naples are so secret, they give the impression of having been deliberately concealed; lodged away, for the most part, in malodorous side-streets, embedded in some squalid recess, they partake of the city's poverty. Rarely do they give the sense, as do the historic sights of other cities, of having died and been resurrected: from that illustrious after-life their own vitality, their capacity for adaptation has excluded them; they are engulfed in their own continuity.

It is the people, not the monuments, of Naples who are

blatantly featured, every face a subject for study — physiognomy evincing, like architecture, here the Spanish influence, there the Arab or the Greek. Civilisation has come upon them like one of their own cataclysms, flowing with ungovernable impetus down channels of its own creation — in some respects total, all-permeating; in others leaving inexplicable areas of innocence, of rusticity. For there would occur, in that immensity of independent actions, incidents that might have taken place in a village, or in some small town cut off from any novelty or tide of history. I remember that one evening I was looking in a shop window in Piazza dei Martiri — at suede shoes of delicate colours, purses of indigo velvet, scarves of satin flowers, Parisian stuff at odds with its southern setting — and turned to find at my back a young couple, modestly though not poorly dressed, the girl in grey, the man wearing a broad black armband. Like a deputation they awaited me, timidly excusing themselves before coming out with their question, "Are you Norwegian?" And, when I was not, excused themselves once more — "Only we heard — you know — that Norwegian women were all fair, and with light eyes . . ."

It was inoffensive curiosity of the kind one might feel on finding a rare bird in one's garden — merely the desire to fix its identity before it disappeared forever. Yet it was, mysteriously, this same simplicity that grandly, gracefully expressed itself in the hairdresser's sturdy little shampoo girl when, sweeping my hair back into the washbasin with her plump arms, she praised its colour and abundance with the comment, *"Come la Maddalena"* — this "Like the Magdalen" as easily uttered as if it had been a flattering comparison with some film star.

The history and geography of calamity had so worked on these people that the excitement attending any public disaster was fundamentally devoid of surprise — if anything, there was an element of relief in the rupturing of an apparently continual suspense. Once, walking in a narrow street (it was Via Carlo Poerio, that has since blossomed into a rank of boutiques but then was strung with greengrocers and *salumerie*, dealers in wrought iron and kapok, and any number of minor junkies), I had crossed to look into an antique shop, when the ground was shaken by a tremendous crash, and I spun round to find that the entire façade of an old palazzo had collapsed into the street, flattening a parked car. From premonition, or from some preliminary sound, I had turned at the very moment of the impact, in time to see the shower of fragments sparking upward in a cloud of plaster-dust. No one was hurt. The car — so instantly and totally crushed that it now appeared to have been like this always — bore on its hollowed roof a heap of mortar, gesso, and masonry, topped by one of the stone garlands that had decorated an upper window and now lay on the summit of the pyre like a wreath on a tomb.

There was an interval of complete, cautious silence before the street's inhabitants came out to look. Far from causing indignation, the catastrophe produced any number of shrugs. *"Che buò?"* they enquired of one another, "What do you expect?" What might be expected, apparently, was just this — that the front of a building might fall off at one's feet. Somebody at last went off to telephone the fire brigade, children started to scale the eminence of masonry and car. When interest had all but subsided, a placid-looking matron revived it by suddenly waving her arms and shrieking, "Danger, danger!" — the word *pericolo* uttered exactly as if it were spelt "breegolu."

It was this sense of catastrophe, impending and actual, that heightened the Neapolitan attachment to life and made an alleviation out of every small diversion or absurdity. The background of adversity, against which all else was to be posed, manifested itself involuntarily in attitude and gesture, in figures of speech, or in the mannerism, habitual as a tic, of warding off the evil eye; in the endless invoking of a patience with which they had been over-endowed in the first place, and which they pronounced almost as if it were the word for madness; in an old woman crying after a boy who had jostled her, "A fine consolation you are."

The city itself was marked by a volcanic extravagance. Its characteristics had not insinuated themselves but had arrived in inundations — in eruptions of taste and period, of churches and palaces, in a positive explosion of the baroque; in an outbreak of grotesque capitals, or double geometrical staircases; in a torrent of hanging gardens poured down over terraces and rooftops, spilt along ledges and doorsteps. The very streets were composed of blocks of lava, dark rivers that flowed through Naples and gave place, indoors, to a sea of ceramic tiles and marble intarsia: the word lava itself, in its volcanic sense, had originated at Naples. The Neapolitan painters had flashed through every considerable edifice of the town, leaving the place awash with Solimenas and Luca Giordanos and Lanfrancos, a flood-tide of decoration that rose over walls and across ceilings. Nothing in moderation might have been the motto of these people; who were yet, like their city, ultimately a secret.

Ordinariness, the affliction and backbone of other cities, was here non-existent. Phrases I had thought universal — the common people, the average family, the typical reaction, ordinary life — had no meaning where people were all uncommon and life extraordinary; where untraceable convulsions of human experience had yielded up such extremes of destitution, of civilisation.

Throughout the city there were inexhaustible sources of this or that — little fonts and geysers of commodity or personality: one street provided all the stringed instruments, another all the holy pictures, another all the funeral wreaths, or the coffins; the Hospital of the Pellegrini was the source of macabre jokes; the Albergo dei

Poveri of the grimmest legends. And on New Year's Eve, in a revolting ritual, every window flung forth its annual accumulation of major garbage, burying the city under tons of broken utensils, plastic ornaments, cracked bottles and empty tins, from which, each January, it was slowly re-excavated by the street cleaners.

After I moved to the Posillipo I employed a girl called Serafina, who came to me each morning and stayed half the day, returning sometimes in the evening, if I had guests. For this slender Serafina, the word was wiry. Her flat figure and reedy arms suggested tough fibres and filaments, her hair was tightly crinkled from the scalp into resilient spirals. Her handsome, Semitic profile never smiled, but full-face she expressed a tenacious, embittered humour. There had been, still was, a husband to whom Serafina had been married at fifteen; who now lived and worked at Salerno. To the question as to whether she ever visited him, Serafina replied with a friction of thumb and finger and *"La grana"* — that the journey was too expensive; but she seldom spoke of him and I think that there was also lack of inclination.

In order to arrive before I left for work, she came very early, and many of our conversations took place through the bathroom door — or as I dressed, carrying my coffee about with me from room to room and searching for my earrings or my shoes. I would call out remarks and questions, and back would come her responses soft and deliberate as in church. She felt herself under an obligation to modify my opinions — as if, as a foreigner, I were not qualified to form definite views, even on the weather. If I commented on the cold, she would reprove me, "Not so bad" or "It's the season for it," and a moment later I would hear her calling out the kitchen window to a workman or a neighbour, "Cold enough to split your nails." If a group of boys played their radio full blast on the landing stage below, Serafina would counter my groans with *"Si divertono, poverini,"* at the very instant that she opened the terrace doors to bawl down at them *"Tant'ammuina!"*

In the same way she was a confusion of experience and naïveté. Product of a one-room upbringing in a family of the *bassi*, survivor of war at Naples, yet she was favourably impressed by the fact that I did not smoke, and shocked that I treated animals as if they were Christians; and would fearfully cross the road when approaching the church that housed the exorcised Devil of Mergellina.

Gianni complained a lot about Serafina, as if in engaging her I had been short-changed on the Neapolitan character. "How did you manage to have the only maid in Naples with no personality? Why don't you get yourself some nice Concetta or Mafalda —" he indicated with both hands what shape this replacement would take — "instead of this length of string? Women can be divided, more or less, into cows and shrews; and the shrews are to be avoided." I wondered if, on one of his trips to my kitchen for ice or soda, he had tried to kiss her and been repulsed.

No amount of female receptiveness could have propitiated Gianni, no revenge appeased him. The story of his mother, who had consigned him at the age of nineteen to a five-year term among the merchants, civil servants, and cannibals of Africa was told again and again, always as if for the first time as the sense of outrage sprang up freshly in his heart. "The diseases, then. The climate, the conditions — I am speaking of thirty years ago. When people say of such a life 'It was murder,' they are only speaking the truth. This *was* murder, she tried to kill me." His eyes would become bright with tears; and I thought of Rimbaud.

Gianni's parents had separated when he was a baby, the mother remaining at Rome with two children, the father sailing for Argentina where he had inherited some property. After the war, his father returned to Italy for the first time, coming from New York to Palermo on a cruise ship, and Gianni went to Sicily to meet him.

"It was damned queer, I can tell you — standing there on the dock thinking you were about to see your father for the first time. And then the odd thing of seeing him *not* as your father but as just another person — in a way that practically nobody ever does see their own parents — as if he were simply an acquaintance one might have made. Getting much the same impression as anyone might get meeting such a man. Thinking of him as somebody one might do business with, someone a woman might love. Oh it was queer, all right. Damned queer."

"What was he like?"

"Good-looking. Bold. Debonair, you might say — courtly. He was over seventy, in marvellous shape. His clothes weren't right — but that was America. He was moved, coming back to Italy. Palermo was terrible then, a heap of rubble. I could tell he was horrified, not having seen war. We went to have lunch at that hotel on the sea, outside the town. It was March, trees were in leaf, flowers were blooming, the sea was blue. He put his napkin over his eyes and cried."

Gianni's father had spent some weeks in Italy and returned to Argentina, where he died the following year.

"Having seen him only in old age, I can't picture him any other way — if I imagine him as a student, or courting my mother, or at my christening, he is always seventy-five years old. I can't help it."

Gianni had one brother, much older than he. "A horror. I haven't seen him in five years."

Something extraordinary was that Gianni never mentioned his wife. Once in a while he would speak of his children, two adolescent boys and a little girl, and I knew from Gioconda that he saw them constantly. But of his wife there was never a word, not even an accidental reference to his former life with her. On the other hand, he often mentioned his mother-in-law, whom he fiercely hated, pointing out a harsh-faced woman in the street as resembling her, or telling me, if I gave a sharp response to one of his admonitions, "You're getting to be like my mother-in-law." I came to wonder whether this mother-in-law was not in fact his own wife in disguise, and if he had transferred to her the character of his wife in order to speak of her so often and in such derogatory terms.

Never mentioning his wife made her seem, inevitably, more secret, more sacred.

Of his work, too, he would speak only indirectly. "This thing," he would say. "This thing that I do." During the war, for example, the air force had set him to making documentary films, "as I had already started, then, to do this thing." Wildly authoritative on every other subject, about his profession he was almost diffident.

Gianni had a way of introducing his stories, setting the scene like a playwright or a poet — or a director of films. "Place des Ternes. 1949. June, cold and wet." Or "Milan, high summer, a city deserted. Via Melzi d'Eril — a boulevard whose trees disappeared in a single night of the war, cut down for fuel: the street now — too wide, too bare, you sense something missing, eliminated. A fourth-floor apartment, shuttered, silent, like all the Sundays of the world combined . . ."

Occasionally these stories led to something more — more, that is, than their foregone conclusion, which was

the conquest of a woman or the exposing of some preten-
sion; and one felt then precisely the same agreeable surprise one feels at an unexpected show of talent during a
trite play.

"1933. Rome, on my return from Eritrea. Glorious, as
if seen for the first time. Wherever I went, wanting to
touch the buildings, their colours like flesh, their contours of civilisation . . . Unforgettable, too good to
last. My firm sent me to Munich to learn German, which
they already foresaw as a useful language — looking
ahead, you might say, though not quite far enough. I
never could learn it, but that's another story. I was
boarded with a family in Munich, the wife half Italian,
the husband German. When I had been there a few days,
utterly lost, bored to death, I went alone one evening to
the theatre. I forget the play. In the interval, something
happened. The lights went up more strongly, people got
to their feet excitedly, began talking, gathered in groups
in the aisles. Armfuls of newspapers were brought in and
passed around. I saw the headline, right across the page:
'ROEHM VERHAFTET.' I hadn't the remotest idea
what it meant. 'ROEHM VERHAFTET.' It was Hitler's
coup, the beginning of a massacre. I couldn't ask anyone,
not speaking a word of German. I knew something terrible was taking place — it was an atmosphere of dread,
the sense of vast calamity that makes itself felt like a
chemical agent, even to those who are cheering it on.

"Well, that was what the whole war was to me. An

unnatural light, the performance suspended, and people milling about in an atmosphere of disaster uttering crucial words that I found incomprehensible. In 1940 I was called up, I went into the air force." Gianni shrugged at me, and added belligerently, "What else was I to do, Not being a hero, you might say, I had to go and fight. I didn't have money to buy my way out, as some did, and you had to be a fascist to get yourself a protected occupation."

*"Figlia mia,"* he would say, laying his hand on my arm or my knee. "I am not yet an old man, and in my time I have lived through —" now raising his hand and striking his fingers one by one — "the war of Italy with Turkey; the First World War; the war of Italy with Ethiopia; Italian intervention in the Spanish Civil War; and the Second World War. I have seen allies alternate with enemies, sometimes within the same war. Are you asking —" (I was not) "that I should continue to take these events seriously?"

When Gianni dealt with matters of this kind — when he told his stories, or sang, or came to grips in any other way with human feeling — he wept. That is to say that his eyes filled, and tears sometimes appeared on his face. He was proud of these tears, making no attempt to conceal or remove them, even exhibiting a little this irrefutable evidence of his tender heart. It was as if he said to us; Well, there you are: you think me callous and egotistical, yet here are the springs of compassion welling up before your very eyes.

But tears are not, like blood, shed by all involuntarily and according to the same determinants. And I had come to wonder, from the cauterized state of my own emotions then, whether those who have suppressed or diverted the course of strong feeling are sometimes left immune, with nothing more than just such superficial traces of what was once a great affliction. If, for instance, at this time when all my faculties seemed blunted — not only by grief and change, but by the very effort of surviving them — if, as I say, I recalled a poem or a piece of music, a choking emotion might prevent me from completing the passage, even in my head; this happened automatically, as if the words or notes were some signal that drew up passionate response without reference to my own sensibilities. I would, uselessly, attempt to arouse the same reaction for a more immediate cause, for my own troubles or for sorrows witnessed: but I was like a person who has come down from a mountain or a long air journey, and is slightly deafened. Yet a line from a sonnet, a phrase from a sonata, drew tears as involuntary as those caused by an onion passed under the nose. And I concluded that Gianni's tears were the refined product of a conditioning that was similar, but self-imposed and lifelong.

Gioconda, for instance, had an astonishing memory for verse — I have never heard anything like it; and would sometimes say lines to us, or whole poems, that were unknown to me: it was through her that the Italian poets entered my consciousness — or, rather, that I entered theirs. It was the one thing in which Gianni allowed her to shine, never interrupting unless to offer a word if she hesitated, sitting back with his hands locked under his head and one foot crossed over the opposite knee. And throughout these brief recitations of hers, he would always weep.

Afterwards, if we went late to dine together, perhaps, in one of the *trattorie* around Piazza Dante, he would — with his eyelids still reddened from crying — drive me crazy by abusing the waiter, sending back the carafe of wine, and criticising Gioconda's dress.

Like many men who are compulsively cruel to their womenfolk, he also shed tears at the cinema, and showed a disproportionate concern for insects.

# ❧ VIII ❧

"I spent most of the war in England. That was the frightening part. It was a relief to get to safety, when they sent me on active service — when I went to Mombasa in '44. Up till then I was getting blitzed at a naval station in the south of England, at Hove. When I was called up I filled out a form. It asked me where I would like to be sent if I had a choice, and I put 'HOME.' Perhaps they mistook the handwriting, because I was sent straight to Hove and got stuck there for three years. Or perhaps some Johnny was having a joke — there were still a few humorous types around in those days. It was the war wiped the smile off our faces once and for all.

"At the very end of it, in '45, they sent me to the Falkland Islands. That was the worst — though it was good for my work, as it turned out . . . There's a freezing wind there that comes straight from the South Pole and never stops blowing. The place has a demeaning kind of desolation, the flat, bleak kind, not dignified by drama. There was one single tree there, a stunted, heel-ing wretch of a tree, that had become the focus of attention — I think we had all transferred our identities to that tree, and its survival in such a place was bound up with our own. There were a few women, Englishwomen who had been stranded there throughout the whole war — war was like a great syphon that sprayed human beings all over the globe; as you know, Jenny. These women were reduced to lining the perishing remnants of their clothes with newspaper . . . Of course no one could get interested in these kinds of hardships, with what had been going on elsewhere in the world. And the worst hardship was exactly that — the knowledge that one's sufferings were of no interest."

When Justin spoke to me in this way I was ashamed to pass it off merely with a word or a look of agreement, and would have liked to recognise his wish of being, for once, serious with me. But he had so accustomed me to flippancy that I scarcely knew how to make the transition with him — and, having made it, might find him already reverted, no longer in earnest, so that my spontaneity was humiliated. More than that, I resented it — that it should be he, always, who set the tone of our relations.

I forget, on this occasion, what I said, but I remember his taking exception to it.

"You tell me I must talk sense, and when I do you dismiss me."

"Having imposed the climate of non-sense, you can't expect to be taken in earnest the moment you ring the bell. You treat me — things — us — lightly, then expect us to reverse ourselves the one time you choose. You want us to be accessible, indefinitely, waiting for your moment of truth. And we can't be."

"His jaw dropped," said Justin, at once relapsing into banter. "It is the price I pay, he said heavily."

I said, "It is one of the prices he pays."

We were walking down a dark street paved in uneven blocks, and had to keep our eyes on the ground — I think that Justin had come with me on one of my shopping expeditions, and we were going to see a church that was on our way home. It was often this way when we talked — we were driving or walking, instead of facing one another in a quiet room, or in a bed. Because of that, anything we had to say was transmitted with involuntary sidelong looks that heightened the glancing, facetious character of our friendship. It might have been different face to face, when expression would have counted, and less would have had to be spelled out, or evaded, in words.

In the church, unexpectedly, there were two or three tourists walking slowly back and forth, their heads prayerfully bowed over guidebooks, like so many Hamlets on their way to encounter Polonius. This also was part of our fate, Justin's and mine — just as we were often in motion during our conversations, so too we were bound to arrive at destinations and to part, or be otherwise distracted. The church itself, a veritable grotto of the rococo, mocked all indignation. I smiled to close the subject — though not quite, for I remarked, "We are always at cross purposes, then."

Justin, looking around at the gilded and encrusted interior that was tipped inwards with its weight of decoration, remarked of it, "Hardly a case of *'less is more'* — would you say?" Then turning to me, "Asyngamy, my dear Jenny," he said; and repeated it. "*Asyngamy*. The inability of two plants to achieve cross-pollination, owing to their unsynchronised development. That is our case — a matter of bad timing, nothing more. It need not worry us." Having reached the altar, we turned and slowly walked back down the aisle. "Since, in spite of this nuptial march you and I are taking, neither of us appears to wish at this time to enter into any cross-pollinatory activities." We paused, looking about us, and he said, "These frescoes are by a painter whose nickname was 'Quick-Work,' did you know that?" and we left the church.

It was an evening of late winter, charged with the smell of wood-smoke, shiny with wet streets. Women came past us, covering their mouths against the mild air with the edge of a shawl or a coat lapel, hauling along short schoolboys with long bare legs. A man came by with his hands in the air, telling his companion, "She was so lovely, he so much in love . . ." There was — as there often was, there — the sense of an earlier time: it was not merely the lack of modernity — the chaste black dresses, a momentary absence of cars, the buildings in their ancient places — but truly as if the city had not caught up, had no interest in catching up, was dawdling in some previous era, the turn of this century perhaps, or of any century.

In silence we climbed a straight street lined with cave-like little dwellings of single ground-floor rooms, each scarcely accommodating its vast bed; each marked by Mussolini twenty years before as unfit for habitation — his incontestable plaque now rotting, half-effaced, on the pitted outer wall. At the top of the street, Justin hailed a taxi.

When we had found our niche in a traffic jam, Justin asked me, "Am I right?"

"About the frescoes?"

"About the cross-pollination."

"Once again, the very way in which you speak about these things affects one's reaction. How could one love —" I saw that he did not like this bold word, and repeated it — "that is, fall in love with, such an exponent of the arm's-length technique?" Infuriatingly, I fell yet again into his way of talking.

"It would have to be, would it, straight from the heart? Someone who would bring you armfuls of flowers, and be cut in pieces for you?"

"That's it."

"A modest enough requirement," he agreed. "You

deserve nothing less, Jenny, a lass like you. And try to get that into your head."

There was something about this that recalled Norah's way of trying to undermine your confidence — "You must *believe* in yourself more," she would say; "If only you *knew* how *in*teresting you are," exhortations with which, by imputing to me an ineptitude of manner, she assigned to herself as always the superior role. For a moment I forgot about Justin, and thought of Norah and how sometimes, when Edmund was away, she would come round in the evening to look over my life, running a metaphorical finger around the edges of my existence to examine it for dust.

"It *is* in my head," I told him. "You forget that love does not come from the head. In fact, some of it gives the impression of being painstakingly mindless." But in saying this I was thinking not of Norah but of Gioconda. It was inconceivable to me that she, who might have commanded anything from life, should be glad of the sort of love that Gianni gave her. In telling me her story Gioconda had said of Gianni, "He saved my life." And there are debts of this kind — if debts they be, since Gianni's intervention was not disinterested, nor was Gioconda's feeling for him solely one of gratitude — that in a literal sense can never be paid; one may have performed a hundred services greater than the original one; yet the initial obligation, being spontaneous and unaccountable, will go perpetually, monstrously, undischarged. Thus the pain that Gianni caused Gioconda was, in her view at least, the sort of remedial destruction one can scarcely complain of — like damage done by the water used to put out a fire.

The taxi had passed through Piazza Municipio, and reached the rise behind the Royal Palace — an intersection which, with the combination of castle, palace, opera house, and arcade, is as close as Naples ever comes to the civic and historic coherence of other large cities: a relief to tourists, and an anomaly to the inhabitants who feel themselves exposed there on that tract of open ground, and tend to avoid it. Justin asked, "Is there a possible restaurant round here? Let's hop out."

"You know they're all terrible." We stopped the car and made our way through the traffic and into the Galleria. Couples milled about us, arm in arm. Justin's hand at my elbow was lifeless, worse than dutiful.

We were early — first, in fact — in the little place where we went to dine. The owner scraped out our chairs for us, crying *"Buona sera, buona sé,"* as if he had hardly expected the pleasure of having customers; as if we were a good omen. Justin shamelessly reproduced the greeting in return.

"Now come Jenny," he said. "Even Shakespeare made fun of the Neapolitan accent." Pouring purple wine into thick, clouded tumblers, he remarked, "The thing is, Jenny. The thing is. Much of what we discuss is currently meaningless to me. Not human affairs alone, but other matters as well. The seasons, for instance — even the seasons bore me . . . And the very word Love which just now you so brashly used — that word is the greatest bore of all to me. At this moment, as one might say, women delight not me."

I thought of his hand on my arm and wondered, was he passionless, perhaps; or effeminate.

"Nor men either, though by your smiling you seem to say so."

The menu came, a limp paper elaborately illegible in mauve ink, enclosed in soiled plastic. We shared it, leaning across our tiny table, and Justin touched his head companionably to mine.

I said, "Certainly what one sees around is not encouraging. The doomed attractions, impossible unions. Though I don't really call those love."

"Then you do wrong, Jenny." For the moment abandoning his quotations, he said, "You are mistaken. All that which you deplore — the blind obsession, the unequal sacrifice, the punishment invited and inflicted — that is love. Believe me. It's pointless to call upon perfect harmonies and deathless romance. For love, you must look closer to home."

We ordered our meal. Justin broke a hunk of bread and gave me half of it. "Those in love — do they ever talk about it in this way — as we are doing, as if it were susceptible of logic? Of course not. It is like the exemplary treaties on whaling — ratified by everyone who is not involved. Those concerned are not signatories, and the whale will be exterminated as a matter of course. I believe the Japanese will knowingly harpoon the last blue whale. Many lovers have given their partners a less merciful end, though all manner of laws and arguments be ranged round to prevent it."

His plate arrived, a dish of rubbery seafood becalmed in red sauce.

I said, "You're too much influenced by your own experience."

"Not the whole story, eh?"

"By no means."

"What do you know about it?" He smiled, but it was an unworthy answer. He wished to conclude, now, this talk of love. He took up his fork and probed the contents of his plate. "Good stuff, this. I most willingly partake of it."

"You try to make me partake of your disillusionment," I said. "However, I don't hold it against you."

"His brow — as they say — cleared."

But when we came out of that place, and started to walk past the palace in the direction of the seafront, Justin reverted to the nature of our friendship. "We are both, to be explicit, at a loss. Isn't that it? Have been deprived of something and are in a state of abeyance. Can afford to be fastidious, having insufficient courage, at present, to be otherwise."

I agreed. Though he was more like someone who has

had an operation and waits to see whether the disease is cured, or mortal. And love not being, as he had just pointed out, rational, might he not at any time have become its victim over again, the more unguardedly for all this interim rationalisation?

Turning into Via Santa Lucia we stopped on the slope to watch the passage of a truck stacked high with refuse, from the summit of which a pair of seated urchins pontifically saluted us.

"Oh Jenny, how will we explain it to anyone, when we get out of here?"

"We never will. No one ever has." We walked on, our shoulders touching.

"I was brought up to think of Naples, if at all, as superstition, sentiment, glee. Yet the other view — that it is all cynicism, gloom, amorality — is just as much a myth, only a more pretentious one. The sort of platitude that calls itself a theory. Simply to know the worst about a place is not to know it. What is it then? Civilisation, curiosity completely satisfied, style, irony, magnanimity . . . Being able to greet the world like a king from the top of a dunghill." We stopped again, at the curb, and looked back up the street, and Justin laughed. "The tourist who comes and sees this shambles, has his camera swiped, is swindled by the taxi drivers and persecuted by old codgers flogging cameos, how can he know all that is just, so to speak, a show of civilities? — the surface pleasantries of a reality which is infinitely worse, unanswerably better?" He put his arm around me suddenly and squeezed me. "Why Jenny," he said, seeing my eyes full of tears. "You old bubblyjock."

"It's nothing," I said. "Only pleasure."

"Call that nothing, do you?" Justin let me go. "So there you are, there is something that moves you. Said he cannily. This place."

"Even that is muted."

"Places take more time than people. There is no real love at first *s-i-t-e*." He spelt it. "Yet with people I do believe in it — instant attraction."

"So do I."

"We can't have our way so much with places."

What kept our odd acquaintance going, Justin's and mine, was something more than the state of suspension that he claimed we shared. It mattered to us both to have some point of reference in that strange place, some means of attesting to the effect it had on us. We used each other as the army wives used the PX — not only as a convenient source of supply, but as a source of the totally and reliably familiar. Between our separations and encounters, the city worked on us; and when we met it was as if to measure, against the supposedly fixed point of the other, the distance it had brought us; to compare, without discussing them, our unwritten notes.

I seldom spoke, for instance, to Gioconda of my brother and his wife. When I did mention them it was usually to Justin. In the first place, Gioconda would have understood too quickly, instinctively, without absorbing the circumstances. An incestuous passion, consummated or otherwise, was an everyday affair at Naples, and she would never quite grasp what recognition of it in myself had meant to me. Whereas Justin saw it against the tweed-and-cretonne background of post-war England and did not discount my distress, even for purposes of giving comfort.

Something else that inhibited me in talking of these matters with Gioconda was the scope and drama of her own tragedies. Whereas the excavations of Gioconda's past brought to light temples, palaces and tombs, with ornate interiors worthy of grand gestures and heroic re-nunciations, my own archaeology seemed by comparison like a mere scouring of some minor site — a hilltop en-campment of the Hittites, say, or some beehive village of the Picts — yielding nothing more than a heap of do-mestic utensils and a handful of weapons, few intact and none beautiful.

Gioconda herself, however, could not bear any sug-gestion of drama in her past. It was one of the few things that discomposed her. "No, no, no, you can't conceive the dreariness of it, the indignity, the crushing daily items of an unhappy life, how endless time is when one wishes it past for no object, when one is continually afraid. I can hardly believe now that the war lasted only five years. One didn't know then how any of it might end, if it would ever end. Now it appears to have had a beginning and a conclusion, but we could not know then the form it would take, and assumed only the worst . . . And the physical hardship — hunger, cold, being dirty, the time wasted searching for food, trying to be clean. Suffering, and the sight of suffering, and the knowledge of the worse suffering that is unseen." And she would spring up and walk about her room.

Gioconda showed anger rarely. But the way in which she avoided certain subjects — government, religion, world events — and made light of other ones suggested the control of strong feeling rather than the absence of it; even, that there was violence in her which she recognised and disciplined, and that whenever this got the better of her, as it occasionally did, she was ashamed. Once, when we drove to Rome in her little car, I remember that we crossed a narrow river-bed, mostly stones; and I, seeing the sign on the bridge, cried out with the memory of the war, "The Volturno — but it's such a little river!" And Gioconda turned to me — turned on me, you might say — and almost shouted, "They were all little rivers, all of them, always. Can't you see that?" When we had driven on she gave an apologetic laugh and glanced at me, and said, "Wait until you see the Rubicon." But for the rest of the journey she was subdued and defensive, as if she had exposed herself and regretted it.

She gave, in talking, a number of these clues to passions that, had she not contended with them, might have ruled her — as when she had described herself writing at her father's deathbed, or when she said to me, "Italians are seldom harmless." But I, having established my own idea of her, was unwilling to let her extend herself into complexities, and disregarded these promptings.

"People resort to violence," she said to us, one evening when Gianni had taken us to dinner, "not to relieve their feelings, but their thoughts. The demand for comprehension becomes too great, one would rather strike somebody than have to go on wondering about them."

I noted the transition from "people" to "one." I could not say I had ever felt the need of striking Norah; but then she was not a person one was required to wonder about.

"In my youth," said Gianni, "I did some amateur boxing. But I would never have made a real *pugilatore*. My guard was too high. I had conceived some idea — mistakenly, no doubt — of my good looks, and I tried to protect my face. Yes, my guard was rather high; and that kept me from being really good."

"What I mean is, in anger. Or in some culmination of resentment."

On the other hand she could not be roused, as almost any Anglo-Saxon can be, to vocal indignation; she sensed its falsity and would have no part of it.

In the warm early spring of that year the garbage collectors of Naples went on strike; their wages had not been paid, due to a disappearance of departmental funds. Rubbish piled up on pavements that were coated with grit, drains were blocked, refuse blew back and forth across littered streets, and one day at high noon I spotted a great ginger rat with prominent teeth hanging about behind the Hotel Excelsior.

"*Una zoccola,*" Gioconda said, when I described it. "That's what they call a rat like that in Neapolitan."

"Well, it's disgraceful."

"The word also means a prostitute — in fact, the saying here is that the last straw for a cat would be to lie in the arms of its mistress without realising that she was *una zoccola.*" Gioconda giggled. "The rat's nest, that's what Leopardi called Naples, *La Topaia.*"

"It's a scandal."

But these matters went too deep with her, she would not be drawn into them casually and merely shrugged to summarise twenty centuries of civic disillusionment.

"What will happen?"

"Oh — they say the mayor will have to pay the garbage-men out of his own pocket, the old devil. He's rich, he owns a shipping line. Whoever took the money kept that in mind, I daresay."

"But Gioconda, what a state of affairs."

"The *scogliere* are full of them — those white rocks, you know, piled up along the shore."

"Full of what?"

"Of *zoccole.*"

The mayor, who was off in Sardinia, flew home and paid the garbage collectors from his private fortune; and Naples was cleaned up in time to hold a series of huge official receptions, in full dress, for a congress of the International Chamber of Commerce.

Conversely Gioconda would puzzle, unpredictably, over matters that I easily absorbed or dismissed. Once in a while she reverted to the manner of our meeting, as if it continued to exercise her. I had written to the young man from Ealing, and forgotten him. But every so often Gioconda would pay him tribute for bringing us together — saying "Think of it" or "How unlikely," as if there were something there to be unravelled. She called him "the Pharmacist," after an episode in a poem of Gozzano in which a great attachment is formed through a chance meeting in a chemist's shop. It was as though she dwelt on these freakish, unresolved influences of our existence, wondering if they were coincidental or supernatural.

Gioconda, moreover, had substance and territory of her own, while I earned a weekly living and was without even those resources that continuity of place and persons might have given me. When she told me how her book had enabled her to pay off the accumulated taxes on her flat, the fact of having a flat to be taxed on, and access to such a solution, made her, for me, a person of means and set her at liberty.

These aspects of independence engendered passivity in me. The conviction from which she expressed herself was too pleasing — too reassuring — for me to challenge it: I took note of her affinities and opinions in a way I had done with no one else.

When she said one day, in talking of my family, "They will recede," I felt assured, from her saying it, that it would be so. "Even your brother. You will think less about him, not seeing him, seeing others."

"My love," I primly answered her, "is not conditional."

She was standing on a chair, putting a book back, and did not look down. "Love is the most conditional thing there is. A word, a tone of voice, a moment's silence can change it irrevocably. I didn't mean your feeling for your brother would completely dissolve. But it will lose its prominence and become a more and more distant landmark."

When she spoke this way I felt more than simply the truth of what she said. It was all natural to me, just as the sounds of Italian had seemed natural when I first began to learn them, and I wished I might always have been with people who thought and spoke like this.

It did not occur to me to remind her of the contradiction in her own case. And what of your love, I might have said, subjected to so many words and actions and silences that might have changed it, and yet apparently immutable?

# ✒ IX ✒

Gioconda spent the month of April on Capri. At Easter I saw her there when, for the long weekend, I too crossed to the islands. She was thinner — or seemed so, in grey trousers and a crimson pullover. The collar of a white shirt rising round her throat made her look at once younger and more womanly.

Gianni was coming down from Rome, reaching the island by the last boat on Good Friday. *"Il vaporetto dei cornuti,"* Gioconda remarked of it, as we watched the boat approaching from Naples. "The boat of the cuckolds. That's what they call it in summer when the rich take houses here — this last boat on Friday that brings the husbands over to join their wives for the weekend."

"With us it would be the other way round. In the summer it's assumed the husbands have been having adventures all week in town."

"That too." Gioconda pleated her ticket, then unfolded it. She was on her way to the port to meet Gianni, and we were waiting for the funicular to take her down.

She was often nervous, now, when Gianni was coming; once he was there she became calm, imperturbably so. "But that's of course. It's the other way round that's significant, humiliating, frightful."

"I don't see it," I said; and she laughed and flicked at me with her ticket, and said, "If you don't see that, you don't see anything."

"Truly, it always seems to me," I said, although I had not considered the matter before, "that women are rather more faithful than men wish them to be."

"You mean that a man will call a woman neurotic if she is faithful one moment beyond the time when he desires her love. When he himself has ceased to love."

I had not meant this, and wondered if she were thinking of Gianni's wife.

"But there again he retains what matters to him — the initiative."

After Gioconda had gone down to the port, I sat at one of the cafés in the piazza, rejoicing in liberty as I had done that December afternoon outside the Hotel Royal. I dwelt with almost physical pleasure on the evening that lay ahead to spend as I wished, with no need to be up early next day to meet the Colonel at the car. As I was enjoying these thoughts, the Colonel came out of the post office in a sports jacket and sat down at my table.

"Enjoying the Isle of Capri, I see." He said it "Ca-pree," as in the song. After a while he said, "You had better have dinner with me." He had this way of expressing himself in unfinished threats.

I submitted to everything, having, as I thought, no excuse for doing otherwise, and not at that time realising that my own preference was a justification. I went to dinner with the Colonel, in a restaurant near the piazza. He talked at length, savagely — and stupidly, for it is stupidity that makes people cruel — about Naples, about Italians, about our colleagues, and about a wider state of human affairs that he identified as "this mess." When he went into the kitchen of the restaurant to complain about his fish, I dropped into his white wine a small sleeping pill I had put in a box in my handbag to be sure of sleeping long on my holiday. And by the time the wild strawberries arrived the Colonel had begun to doze.

Recounting my evening to Gianni and Gioconda in the piazza next day, I spotted the Colonel blearily reading his newspaper. (He could not know the whole cause of our laughter, but must have sensed the trend, for the following week he kept me late at work each evening for no purpose. He never came to Capri again, so far as I know, and often spoke of it as being full of degenerates.)

I noticed too that Gianni, who had flung himself back in his chair with a roar of delight at my story, became quieter at the sight of Gioconda with her hand to her mouth and tears of laughter brimming over her eyelids. It made him uneasy, not only the revelation of female duplicity, but her pleasure in it. Weeks later, when the Colonel cropped up in some other connection, Gianni went so far as to say that he felt "sorry for that man, with all you women baiting him."

Gianni had hired a small boat in which he proposed to row us to an inlet, away from the holiday crowd. That morning on Capri we bought a picnic in the sooks of the town, and I got a bathing suit, not having known it would be warm enough to swim. Straddling a chair in a white shop that hotly smelt of the next-door bakery, Gianni pointed out the costume that would suit me best and, to punish me for having got the better of the Colonel, made a scene when I almost chose another.

As we came away he told me, "There you are. Stop sulking. You got the one that'll look best on you."

"That's beside the point," I said, enraged by the uproar he had made.

Gianni stared. "It's the *only* point," he said.

Taking us to the beach to claim the boat, he imagined himself, so it seemed, in possession of every lovely woman we passed. "Legs like that — my God" or "I've always fancied women with that curly, carrotty hair" — in each case his admiration was unrelated to, undiminished by, those that had gone before or would immediately come after. It was something of the same spontaneous and faithless pleasure with which Gioconda herself would remark of almost any flower that she saw — iris or freesias, roses or ranunculus, wild or growing in a pot or gathered in sheaves on a barrow — "That's my favourite flower."

Gianni took credit for the island, as he had done with Herculaneum — for the Judas trees in bloom, the limestone peaks and dolomitic escarpments, the sea luridly streaked between slopes of oak and juniper. Foreign tourists were doing their best to ruin it — "When I knew it first there was one car on Capri, one only, and it belonged to Ferrari."

He told me that Capri had been taken by the English during the Napoleonic wars, though not for long, thank God — "Otherwise, can you imagine? — another little Malta."

Gioconda and I floated in the boat while Gianni swam beneath us, monstrous in a rubber mask.

"That great rock in the sea, the one all by itself. On that the Romans built a funeral pyre for a follower of Augustus Caesar." Gioconda pointed, and I shaded my eyes to look. "The Monacone, they call it, because a monk lived there in the time of Tiberius."

"A monk, in the time of Tiberius?"

"I mean a priest, a *sacerdote* — whatever they had then. So they say, anyway. Gianni and I climbed to the top of it once — there's a hole through the middle of it, like a chimney. You can squeeze up, planting your feet on the sides."

"It sounds awful."

"So it was. The whole thing was somewhat awful — there was no place to land there from the boat, only a jagged shelf covered with sea-urchins. Then this vertical tunnel, wet, black, maggotty . . . On top, though, it was nice — like a big rough tabletop, covered with stunted bushes and flat, circular nests of sea-birds. But going up was horrible. I thought I was going to fall back through the rock and be killed."

"Why ever did you do it?" I asked her, knowing well enough.

"Oh — to be companionable, you know. I'm unathletic, in general, for a person like Gianni."

I could imagine it all — the abuse, the remonstrances, Gianni shouting, "*Su, su, idiota* — not like that, don't you know anything about climbing . . ." At that moment Gianni surfaced alongside. Holding on to the boat with one hand he blew out his snorkel and shook the water from his goggles.

"What a pair — lolling here while there's all this to be seen below. It's marvellous down there. I don't know what's the matter with you."

Gioconda leant over, took the goggles from him and dried them on a towel. Gianni floated on his back beside the boat.

"See that rock, Jenny — I got Gioconda to the top of that one day. What a job. It's marvellous up there. Beautiful, isn't it, Gioconda?"

She agreed.

"All kinds of plants, flowers, coloured lizards. Like a desert island. If it hadn't been for me she would never have been up there."

We had our lunch among the rocks, on an arrow of sand that, once the boat was beached there, scarcely allowed us to stretch ourselves in its shadow. Gianni sang and complained by turns as we unpacked paper cones of fruit and cheese. When we had eaten he lay down in the sun beside Gioconda; but, with his hand shading his eyes, watched me while I sat up recorking bottles and pushing garbage into a bag.

"Jenny," he said. "You really do have a cat's eyes. Amber, are they? Or topaz?"

I told him, "My sister-in-law says they're yellow."

He nodded. "That's the sort of remark I get about my Maserati. Envy makes people desperate." He yawned. "These flies. That's the trouble about being on holiday, you can never rest. You never really take your afternoon snap, as the English call it."

I looked at Gioconda, who lay with eyes closed, as wakeful as he. Sand had dried on her arms and legs, and salt was whitely grained into her brows and lashes. Years later at the Piraeus I saw an Athena, one of two great bronzes that had been lifted intact from the excavations of a drain, lying flat on a stone floor with clay-caked eyes, bringing to my mind Gioconda as she lay motionless near the Saracen Beach that afternoon.

While I watched she opened her eyes. Turning on her side towards Gianni and raising herself on one elbow, she laid her other hand almost tentatively on his midriff. "My God," she said, "you're roasting. You'll be developing the bronze disease."

He had been so petulant, so unpredictable, that day,

with each of us, that I should not have been surprised to see him brush her hand away; and was almost embarrassed when instead he tenderly covered it with his own. "I'm told that goes away with handling," he said.

Gioconda's hair, which floated around her when she swam, falling like a stain over her shoulders or drifting about her like some fringed sea-plant, was bound now to one side in a single thick cable.

"Quite a dish," a youth had remarked, passing us that morning in the street.

"Which one?" asked his friend.

"The Long Plait," the boy replied.

"*La lunga treccia,*" I echoed now, as Gianni reached up and ran the heavy damp pigtail through his hand. "It's what used to be called tresses."

"Yes," said Gianni. "The sort of hair people could cherish locks of."

I told them how, on one of my sister-in-law's excursions to the inner circle, I had gone to John Murray's in London and been shown the locks of hair clipped by Byron from his loves. "On one he had put 'Whose it is I do not recollect. But it is of 1812.' Then there was one — identified by Byron as something like 'Lisbon, 8–10 P.M., October 17th' — incredibly long, coarse, straight, almost like a horse's tail."

"How Byronic," said Gioconda, "in the truest sense, if he had clipped a horse's tail and had it reverently preserved by his publisher as a souvenir of the Romantic era."

Gianni said, "I can think of a still more Byronic explanation, but decency forbids." With his free hand he killed a sandfly that had settled on his stomach, and remarked, *"Un salaud de moins.* Byron," he went on, rubbing his palm in the sand to clean it, "Now there's a great man. You know, he wrote to his friend, 'My mother-in-law has been dangerously ill, and now is dangerously well again.' " He passed the heavy braid of Gioconda's hair through his hand again, allowing her enough rope.

She leant away from him, laughing, letting him hold the taut pigtail by its tip. "I'm at the end of my tether," she said.

One wet morning at the beginning of May, Germani, our driver, made known to the Colonel and me a Neapolitan saying — "Rain on the fourth of May, rain for four weeks." As this cheerless maxim, possibly invented on the spur of the moment to distract our attention from some near miss to a barrow or a bicycle, proceeded to fulfill itself to the letter, the Colonel's daily greeting to me was transformed from his unintelligible rendering of *"Buon giorno"* into "Sunny Naples." And there he would stand, day in, day out, in a dripping doorway on Via Posillipo, saying "Sunny Naples" to himself and me and never tiring of it — so relieved was he to be confirmed in his suspicion that the fame of Naples was groundless and that he need not trouble himself over its origins. Through the words one could retrace his military past, picturing the successive theatres of service in which he had snorted "Sunny Spain," or "Sunny Egypt," or "Sunny Palestine," as the spring rains poured down on him in absolution.

In the third week of that month, as we stood, the Colonel and I, looking over a rucked and slatey sea to the blurred cone, rising on its buff-coloured pediment of habitation, I was opening my mouth to forestall this observation of his when Justin Tulloch's car drew up beside me, followed by the Vehicle.

"Just in time," I told him, climbing in.

"That's what they called me at school."

"What?"

"Justin Time."

"That man sends me up the wall."

"They called my brother Ethelred the Unready."

"Is his name Ethelred? Really?"

"No. It was just to make a pair of us. Symmetry is not constructed out of logic. Come for a drive."

"You know I can't. I'm late already."

"He's later than you are," said Justin, swerving out and passing the Vehicle. Just as it had been easy to imagine him a Scottish Nationalist, so too I could picture him with the hectic cheeks and plunging walk of the British schoolboy.

"Now Jenny," Justin said to me. "Know this. I grow to be quite fond of you."

"Listen." I touched his knee. "Don't grow to be anything of the kind."

"Listen," he said, copying the gesture but leaving his hand on my knee. "As yet I ask nothing." He went on at once, "On our left, the tomb of Virgil." The car slowed down to merge with the morning traffic of the tunnel that led out of Naples. "Fittingly placed at the gates of Bagnoli." He said, "Good old Virgil. I salute thee, Mantovano." Removing his hand from me he raised it before him, to the great interest of a young man who drew alongside us in a dented Topolino. "About my middle name, now — Jenny, why do you never show any curiosity about my middle name?"

"Well, what is it for heaven's sake?"

"That P — for whose meaning affection would have prompted you to enquire long ere this — that P, my dear, stands for Pericles, a figure for whom my father's admiration knew, as the saying goes, no bounds."

"It's nice. I hope you're not joking."

"I'm not joking. I like it myself."

"I knew someone at Cape Town whose middle name was Vercingétorix, for the same reason."

"I'm jealous of him already."

"Don't be. He's twelve."

This sort of talk could continue through the tunnel and out the other side, past blocks of fascist sport pavilions and *dopoguerra* housing, until Justin left me at my office. "Yabbling away," Justin himself used to call it. I suppose we both knew that something would come of it eventually — felt that it was up to circumstances, having brought us together in the first place, to draw conclusions from so much banter. My own detachment, so far as it was pleasantly conscious, continued to interest me; Justin's, of course, was merely exasperating.

Some time before this I began to have weekends to myself — that is, I could leave the office at lunchtime on Saturday and need not return to it until Monday morning. I made short, rainy trips — down to Paestum, over to the islands, up to Rome. In Rome that May the weather was better. Mostly I went up by train, but Gioconda several times drove to Rome to visit Gianni, and once or twice took me along in her car — a tearing, hooting journey among fields yellow with mustard and trees damp with rising sap; among the little clouds of the olives and the lyre-shaped ranks of budding vines.

They were a relief, those trips to Rome. In the south the rain had begun to dilute our spirits. Even my sister-in-law had read of it in *The Times*, and wrote, "What a shame you are having such frightful weather." In Naples we had given up looking for wedges of clear sky or diagnosing signs of change. At Bagnoli we dodged from building to building tenting our heads with raincoats, and on one of the cameo-hunting expeditions to town I bought a pair of gumboots in Via Roma, at a shop that called itself the Fountain of Rubber. At first merely a symptom of the sirocco, the rain was now being attributed to the atomic bomb, as if so maddening a phenomenon must of necessity be man-made. In the middle of May the British obligingly detonated a hydrogen bomb in the Pacific, and this — though coming after weeks of rain — was taken as proof by the faction that supported the theory of the *bomba atomica*.

"For all I know," I said to Gianni, "they may be right."

Gianni looked pained, and raised his palm at me like a traffic policeman. *"Figlia mia.* At the end of the First World War, when I was a boy, there was a lot of bad weather in Europe. And why was that? It was the guns on the Western Front, they said; it was the disturbance in the atmosphere caused by poison gas; it was — I forget what other fantasies. Then there was the rain in Italy in '44 — that was due to the bombardment too, as I recall. Now it's the atomic bomb, is it? Let us congratulate ourselves, my dear. It may be that the least we have to fear from shelling, gas, or the atomic bomb is a shower of rain."

Rome was a relief, most of all, from poverty. As Gioconda had said, the collective indigence of Naples bore down sometimes in a begrimed and desperate sadness that all the city's compensations could not outweigh. Rome, poor as it was — poorer then than now — could never crush you with its poverty as Naples did; alleviated by well-groomed, floodlit monuments, by tourism, by a middle class, and by the opulence of church and state, it could never convey the same sense of unremitting daily hardship. I loved, then, these excursions into the comparative well-being of the Romans — the evidence of comfort or of luxury glimpsed through the windows of apartments and displayed in the velvet vitrines of dress shops or art dealers or jewellers. I enjoyed the multiplicity of restaurants and bookshops, the paucity of beggars; it was a pleasure to sit outdoors at a café without watching the envelope of sugar disappear from my saucer into the lightning grasp of a ragged infant. (The few outdoor cafés of Naples likely to provide such refinements as separate, sealed sugars were haunted by these swift children in the way that, at Rome, the restaurants were patrolled by cats.) After the impoverished provinciality with which, at Naples, individual sophistication was invariably countered, Rome — though with its own, less vital brand of provincialism — seemed grandly cosmopolitan to me.

One Sunday morning I sat having coffee beside one of the kiosks in the Borghese Gardens and, in this mood of relief, watched — as if I could never get enough of it — husbands and wives and children, fresh from Mass, washed, starched, and ironed, in white shirts and pink dresses and hats heavy with flowers; accompanied by well-fed babies in high-sprung prams and little silky dogs on red leather leashes. So many of these comfortable, comforting, boring families that one might have imagined there was nothing else in Rome — nothing more distressing, nothing more interesting.

Gianni's apartment was at the top of an old house near Piazza del Popolo, with a long, tawny view of Rome. It was a beautiful and, to me, disturbing place. The rooms were white, and plate glass had been let into some of the deep walls. There were teak tables in front of long sofas, and leather chairs beside Swedish telephones; a high fidelity system was concealed in the bar. Along with this went a pair of eighteenth-century tables in scagliola and a French mirror almost as high as the high room where it hung. There were walls of books, and paintings by Morandi and Derain. In a recess between two windows there was an Attic vase on which Hector and Menelaus contended for the body of Patroclus. In Gianni's bedroom there was a great picture: a landscape seen through tears of joy.

I had never seen such things in a private house until then (for my expeditions with Norah had broken off just as she was entering her great collections phase), and was much moved by them. Gianni, curiously enough, took less credit for my pleasure than he had done at Capri or Herculaneum, quite modestly asking, "You really like it then?" or saying, "You know he painted several versions of this."

There was a study, other bedrooms — I don't think I ever saw all the rooms in Gianni's flat. When I said this to him he answered, "In Italy one should try to have some rooms one doesn't have to enter. Like undeveloped aspects of one's personality."

I never saw a sign of children, not even a photograph. But once on Gianni's crowded desk I saw stamps, torn off and put aside in a pile, as if for a child.

The beauty of this flat of Gianni's was the most troubling of his inconsistencies. It reflected not only an unfeignable degree of intellect and feeling, but even — for its main impression was of clear surfaces, of space without ornament — a certain austerity of temperament: qualities that one must exclude from Gianni's composition in order to make his daily self comprehensible. Unlike the abrupt suggestions of discord in Gioconda, Gianni's incompatibilities were disturbing in an expansive, favourable sense — like the wide, modern light that came into his rooms from the window-surgery he had performed on that ancient building.

I liked him better on this home ground of his — he was kinder and less dictatorial there; and, with Gioconda, even loving.

Just then it was as though he could not let her out of his sight. If she went on to his terrace or disappeared into another room (and she wandered about that place pulling out books and touching plants like a nosy child that seeks, in strange surroundings, the sources of home), he would shout her name; and at once she would call back to him, "*So' qua,*" or appear in a doorway, "*Eccomi.*" I remember that they had asked me to lunch one Sunday — it was that Sunday of the Borghese Gardens — and Gioconda went out of the room to fetch something from her coat or her handbag. Gianni suddenly got up from the table and went after her; and in that long mirror that went from floor to ceiling I saw him take her in his arms without a word.

The apartment was open for business at all hours. Even on Sundays the phones were ringing and people were let in and out carrying briefcases and big flat portfolios. Gianni had a secretary, a soft, quiet, humorous man called Bindi who wore glasses (he had a chronic eye infection) and was prematurely bald. Bindi's pink-rimmed, unshockable appraisal missed nothing. Since he was always present, always overworked, I assumed he lived in the building; but later found out that he had a wife and many children and an apartment of his own quite far away, near Piazza Bologna. It was hard to see how he had contrived to create these ulterior circumstances.

At night there were always friends who dropped in — screenwriters, actors, businessmen, foreigners who lived in Rome, and a great many women. These women of the film world were fascinating to me. I was hypnotised by their lifted hair (hair then was beginning to be teased, though not yet into those conical towers that were to be erected the following year), or curled sideburns sleekly flattened to the cheek, their marvellously pencilled eyelids, and silvered lamé breasts deflecting, like so many armoured plastrons, any remark not exclusively concerned with themselves. There were other women, too, brought by men and no less notable in their capacity for total preoccupation with a new scarf or bracelet, and in their total incuriosity regarding the world — or even the room — around them. Their white-blonde or blue-black heads carried high, never inclining to any expressive attitude, they reminded me — as they stood about on Gianni's terrace or his Persian rug — of those columns that support the mosque at Córdoba, each with its diversified capital, serving extravagantly to show how many varieties of a single object can be put to a common purpose.

Coming from an upbringing and a society in which at that time even married couples — or, rather, especially married couples — affected to ignore their sexual connection, or to treat it as something apart and almost irrelevant to their shared life, I liked to see the forthrightly sexual pairing of woman with man. On the other hand, it struck one that the women were required only to be vain, and the men to be proud, any attributes beyond these being unlooked-for, and not always welcome. Their talk was like their appearance — well expressed and without intellect.

"What did you expect?" said Gioconda, when I remarked on this. "Italians don't say interesting things — everyone knows that. You're not in Paris, after all." This circle of Gianni's exasperated her.

In one way, though, their talk affected me with homesickness, for I envied the intimacies of language and upbringing, all the puns and jokes and local allusions that even such a gathering as this could generate — and in which I could never truly participate even were I now to live among them always. These regional code-words should come forth naturally or not at all, if one is not to sound over-accommodating in one's own ears. The American in England who treats himself to an occasional broad A and talks about draught Bass, the Englishman who in Paris takes up gallic mispronunciations of English words, abjectly relinquishes his identity without gaining an authentic substitute; thus in Naples I could not speak of Via Roma by the old name — Via Toledo — by which I had never known it, though to everyone else it might be the "Tuleto."

It was of course the very game of language that with Justin I resisted — because in his case I felt that it was being played against me.

Of Gianni's colleagues, or collaborators, or rivals, whom I met there — men whose names, like his own, were associated with the post-war films, I could rarely get him to say a good word: their work was "*sciocchezze*" or "*cafonaggine*"; this one had run out of ideas, that one had become a megalomaniac, another was an imbecile.

"But Gianni, he seems a literate man, at least."

"As long as you don't talk to him about literature." Or "Nothing special," he would declare. "As the English say, very run of the mile."

Gioconda took me to see her own friends in Rome — a

young antiquarian, an ancient physicist, a prolific nov-
elist, and a journalist who almost succeeded in shaming,
on one or two occasions, the Government of Italy with
his pitilessly documented revelations. I remember how
we went, she and I, to faceless modern buildings near
Piazza Vescovio or off Via Salaria and squeezed ourselves into tiny lifts that ascended, shuddering, to these
shrines where the high priestess — wife, mistress, or
mother, always beautiful, always anxious — would
usher us down the dim corridor to the darkened sanctum
murmuring her warning, "X is a a bad mood today" or
"You will find Y a little distraught" (these women invariably referring to the object of their devotion by the
single last name). X or Y, sunk in gloom, immobile as
the Buddha, sometimes suffering the intrusion with
barely a greeting, would receive our opening remarks
with an expression of excruciating *ennui*. The first morose, monosyllabic responses, like the heavy, separate
drops preceding a great storm, would be followed at
length by the inundation — castigation of the government, of the church, of modern art, modern literature,
modern Italy: "Italians hate beautiful things — look
how they are destroying Rome," X or Y would thunder,
gripping the arm of his ugly modern chair or pounding
his plywood table. Or "They worry about the bandits in
Sicily, but the real bandits are in Rome, sitting in Par-
liament." "As to the *Front Populaire* . . ." With out-
moded expressions they expounded dated causes — or

was it we who were more and more successively dated, passing from one timely issue to the next, while they had remained constant, unfashionably, untopically altruistic?

The ultimate impression they made was of innocence — the novelty of passions not yet turned to slogans, of gifts not deployed for gain, of goodwill not turned to self-importance. Artists, then, had not yet begun to talk of their influence, nor journalists of their artistry. When he spoke, X or Y, wistfully of New York or Paris or London, as places where one could be free of cliques and jealousy and parochialism, one could only feel protective towards this moving belief in the existence, on the earth, of some wider and loftier society in which human nature was represented only by its virtues.

Of them Gioconda said to me, "They don't have to justify themselves, and that gives them less to talk about than other people. In the war we all had to choose, there are no hypothetical positions left to be taken. In this country, everything has been demonstrated. That's why the talk is often about trivialities — who has the *malocchio*, who is stingy, who is homosexual; whereas in other countries people can go on talking out their moral positions on the assumption they will never be called on to live up to them by sacrificing their means, or their standing, or their children, or their lives. These friends of mine are rather disliked for having done the right thing. And for choosing obscurity afterwards."

Another time she told me, "I think that's why films

were such a big thing in Italy after the war. It was something fresh, untainted — an art whose practitioners hadn't as yet disgraced themselves."

All these friends of Gioconda's were men. And watching them lean forward to talk to her, to bend over her hand as she arrived, or embrace her on her departure, I would think any one of them more eligible than Gianni to be her lover.

# ❧ X ❧

JUNE CAME, and there was no more rain. Gianni was making a film at Tripoli — "One of those films, you know," Gioconda told me, "that take place in Siberia but are filmed in Africa." He was to be there some weeks, and wanted Gioconda to come down for a while before it got too hot. He wrote that there was a plane to Tripoli from Naples once a week.

"Why should Gianni want to make a film like that?" On some days I was more unkind to her about Gianni than on others.

"I suppose he wants to get rich," she said, as if it had no more meaning than if she'd said, "For his health" or "For a joke." Gianni, apparently, had not chosen obscurity. She went on about the journey: "It would only be for ten days or so." We were sitting in the sun at a café on the seafront of Naples, and it was the first fine weekend of that summer. She put Gianni's letter away in her handbag. I could see she wanted to go.

"Of course you ought to go," I urged her, giving the right response. "It'll be fascinating."

"What will be fascinating?"

"Oh — Roman ruins, all that."

She smiled. "One doesn't leave Italy to see Roman ruins. Then there's all that crowd —" She disliked the prospect of appearing there as Gianni's mistress. Still she wanted to go. "I'll have to have a dress made."

She and I had coffee together again, on the day of her departure. I was bringing some documents to the airfield that noon, and we arranged to coincide. Arriving hot and nervous in a taxi, Gioconda joined me in the civil airport, at a little bar that no longer exists, and we waited for her flight to be called. She put perfume on a handkerchief and touched her ears with it, the scent at once evaporating into the smell of espresso and of the solution used to wash the terrazzo floors. She was more agitated than I had seen her. She had been delayed at the hairdresser — her too rigidly dressed hair was strained back and lacquered; her brow was pink and shiny from the electric dryer. She was wearing, for the first time, a suit quite matronly in its self-effacement, its good sense. It hurt me to see this suit with its instinctive repudiation of her position (a wife, I suppose, might have decked herself out like a courtesan for such a reunion). A gesture of pressing her forehead, then tucking the handkerchief into her sleeve was prim, even spinsterish.

I was moved, too, to see her excited as a child — but

no, for there is no childhood excitement to equal the adult journey to the beloved.

She held out her hands to me over the coffee cups. "My nails. There was no time to have my nails done."

I see her, upright in that pale linen suit, holding her hands out over the stained table.

"It will be the first thing he'll notice."

"Then he won't be very observant." Childishly, I could not bring myself to send love to Gianni.

"I'll send you a card, Jenny. Of the Roman ruins."

When her flight was called and we embraced, I felt anxiety — that the plane might crash, that something else might go wrong. I felt as if I were being let down: nothing connected with Gioconda had ever seemed inauspicious until this. For the instant of our farewell, the roles were reversed and I was playing her protector. I watched her pass through a railed enclosure banked by eucalyptus, and across a field of glittering concrete to the plane. Her thoughts already on Gianni, she did not look back and wave.

That day was the beginning of a heat wave that lasted till Gioconda's return. The days were hot at dawn. My bed faced double doors that gave on to the terrace, and I would be wakened at five by rails of scalding light that spilt through the shutters. When I looked out the sea would be still as a lake, the sky blindingly red, and the volcano against it black and enormous. Serafina, arriving from a sleepless night, had always the same cynical gesture of supplication, and the same remark to make about the heat — *"Da morire. Un caldo da morire."*

Combinations of colour flared out, in spontaneous combustion, like fires all along the Posillipo — plumbago and oleander, bougainvillea heaped on vermilion walls: the sun made everything possible. Germani had flowered too, as at a signal, into large, shockingly white shoes that came above his ankle. In the car he kept a tube of cleaner with which, at stop lights, he was forever furtively chalking off small blemishes from these feet of clay.

The Colonel, who had given up "Sunny Naples" just when it would have meant most, was revelling in his new disenchantment: he had been in the tropics, in the desert, in the jungle, so it turned out, without ever experiencing worse heat than this. "But *there*," he would say as we stood in the shade of the *portone*, or perspired in our boiling car, "there life was arranged for it, they knew how to handle it. Here they haven't a clue."

In the evenings it seemed that each window of Naples framed some pale woman or trio of exhausted children leaning out for air. The waterfront, the park below the palace, every street in the city was a refuge from rooms that heated throughout the long day; and the population of Naples walked about all night, unsurprised, as if of all their afflictions this was the one they were most prepared for. Small boys with over-large, over-knowledgeable Neapolitan heads trotted up Via Chiaia on bare feet, wearing wet bathing slips and carrying here a fishing rod improvised from a curtain rail, or there a float consisting of a patched inner tube.

A week after Gioconda's departure a postcard came from Tripoli — the arch of Marcus Aurelius in pink and yellow, with a chartreuse minaret in the background. "Roman ruins, just as you said," Gioconda wrote, and concluded, "So here we are — *enfin.*" "Killing heat," Gianni had added. *"Un caldo da morire.* Be glad you're in Italy where they know how to handle it." I wondered about *"enfin."*

A second card — Sciara Adrian Pelt from the Castle — showed a flat and windy shore, office buildings, and a corniche lined with palms. "Back no later than the 18th," and Gioconda had signed herself *"tua Gioconda."* Underneath was scrawled, *"Bacetti — tuo Giannino."*

Gioconda came to see me one evening, a week or so after her return. I was just back from work when she arrived and was changing my dress. On the way home I had bought a carton of milk at the PX. For hygienic reasons this milk was brought down from a NATO installation in West Germany, where its waxed container had never entertained the possibilities of Neapolitan high summer: in the heat of the taxi the container melted entirely away, leaving the floor of the car awash with purified milk. I consoled the stupefied driver with banknotes and squelched into my flat a few minutes before Gioconda came to the door.

She was deeply sunburnt, to a high colour that flushed her cheeks and burnished her hair. She wore an immaculate white dress, a dress that no one would launder for themselves. Because of the milk I had come to the door in bare feet, and she seemed to me statelier and taller than before. She laid down on my hall table a wide hat of stitched blue linen she had carried in her hand.

She stretched out on a long chair on my terrace, saying little, turning her head against the cushions to look at the bay, languidly, like a convalescent. Crowds of children were swimming off the rocks along the Posillipo, or from packed rowing-boats, shrieking at one another in summer ecstasy; every evening they shrieked there as long as the light lasted. Turning on their backs, kicking frantically, they sometimes looked up to us and waved, and she waved back or called out *"Ciao,"* while I set out a jug and glasses on a table between us.

She leant forward to slap at an insect on her bare leg. Along her shoulders, above the back of the dress, the skin was peeling in white flecks. The imperfection was a relief, making her beauty human, vulnerable.

"When it gets dark, I've got a candle that keeps the insects away. A chemical thing."

"What a good idea. Where did you get it?"

"At the PX." I told her the story of the milk.

She laughed, and her own laughter seemed to enliven

her. She looked at the city and at the sea. "What a good place to be."

"And Tripoli?" I asked her.

She spread her hands.

I filled our glasses. "Do you wish you hadn't gone?"

"If I hadn't gone, I would have had to wonder whether I ought to have gone. Something else would have happened — gone wrong — and I would have wondered if it was my fault for *not* going . . . The thing is — one shouldn't have to wonder this much about everything." She took her cold tumbler in both hands and looked over it at the sea. "Ah Jenny, I beg your pardon. I am always telling you my sagas."

"Tell me the Tripoli saga, if you like."

"It was awful. *Ciao, ciao, divertiti!*" She lifted her hand to the shriekers and splashers. "Awful. Oh God, do you remember when we said goodbye at the airport and I was going on about my fingernails? Well, that's how it began." To my surprise she began to laugh again, shaking her head. "Disastrous. That plane stopped at Malta, supposedly for an hour, and I went off to look for a place — a hairdresser's or something — in the airport there that would do those bloody nails of mine for me. There wasn't one — or if there was I never discovered it. But in the meantime they must have called the flight early, and it took off without me."

"Oh no." My hand went to my mouth in her own gesture.

"Yes yes yes. When I found it had gone — Oh Jenny, I tell you. It seemed so much worse at the time too. Isn't it exactly the kind of nitwitted thing that women get the name of doing? — I was furious with Gianni for terrorising me about things like fingernails and for turning me into the sort of person to whom this could happen. Well, it wasn't so bad — fortunately there was another plane to Tripoli within the hour, by mere chance. It was a private affair, chartered for some congress of economists, but I flung myself on their mercy and very kindly they took me with them."

I imagined the delight of the kind economists. It was the sort of thing only an innocent might have done, someone who had not taken the sacrament of officialdom.

"So I got to Tripoli, and there was Gianni at the airport. By then the other plane had come in without me, and he was raising hell with the airline . . . He was so astonished to see me that we didn't even greet one another, just stood and shouted questions. When he heard what had happened — you can imagine."

At this "you can imagine," with its first reference to my own idea of Gianni, its first suggestion of complicity, I felt the compunction one feels when one has ultimately converted — corrupted — another to one's point of view at the expense of some deep conviction of their own. With this phrase Gioconda acknowledged not only my reservations about Gianni, but their validity as well: there was no gratification in getting my own way; only, much graver, more crucial, the pang at her surrender.

"I was this, I was that, it was the temperament of the Mezzogiorno, undisciplined thinking, no thinking at all . . . We drove to town in an open car, and people looked at us — you know, Gianni shaking his fist into the air and roaring *'Paresse mentale! Paresse mentale!'* "

We had both ceased to laugh.

"After that, it never righted itself. He had committed himself to being exasperated, and I to apologising. I could think only of boring things to say, I looked wrong, felt I had brought the wrong clothes — how infantile it sounds — the things we did turned out badly and I felt responsible, even for the heat . . . Everything I did seemed to be the last straw for Gianni. One day he said to me, 'You would understand me better if I spoke Chinese to you.' I thought it would never end." Turned from me in the dying light, her profile was regal, uplifted, oddly matched to what she was saying. But she suddenly looked round at me with eyes of grief. "Oh Jenny," she said in a lower voice, "for the first time I had to wonder — I mean, to fear — what it might be like if I *were* to marry him."

She rested her head back on the cushion and closed her eyes to suppress tears. She added, "Some of it was my fault." She dealt herself a swift, punishing blow on the temple and said, "Mosquito." Then "Maybe Gianni is right," allowing him the last word. "I'm becoming the sort of woman who misses aeroplanes, and recounts her grievances."

I lit the insect-repelling candle and put it on the table.

Gioconda lay with her arms by her sides, not opening her eyes, her body relapsed as an animal's. Over the end of the wicker chaise-longue her sunburnt feet were extended in delicate blue sandals, the toenails painted pink. These well-tended feet looked — as she lay there in pain — pathetic, irrelevant, furbished for pleasures from which she had been drastically diverted; as they might have looked had she been lying on a stretcher after an accident.

Music came up to us from a cockle-shell strung with coloured lights and headed out to Marechiaro. The accordionist was squashed in the stern among lovers, cousins, and aunties who rocked out and in with the rhythm of his arms in a form of collective respiration, and sang whatever was played. As soon as the song was finished they sent up their shouts for others.

"It is so good to be home," Gioconda said. She sat up. "Let's drive to Marechiaro and have dinner. If the car's still there, that is, for I parked in a forbidden place — in conformity, I suppose, with the new role of female nit-wit."

While I was carrying the tray to the kitchen I heard her come inside. When I returned I found her seated at the dressing-table fixing the tortoise-shell comb into the coil of her hair and singing the song that had come up to us from the boat —

> *"Those who are right,*
> *Let's admit they're right;*

*As for those who are wrong —*
*Let's admit they're right too . . ."*

As I watched she rested her fingertips on the table's edge and sat looking into the mirror. I saw in the poise of her head something I had not noticed before — that she had come to hold herself steady, in the way that long-suffering women do, so that you can practically see the blows that have been rained on them, to which they have not bowed, that they have disciplined themselves to withstand. This staunch, dedicated attitude saddened me the more for having about it the expectation and acceptance of future suffering.

When she saw my reflection, however, she sprang up and came over, skating across the tiles like a child. "What a good floor for sliding on. It's the glaze. It looks like a quilt." It was true — the tiles were diamond-shaped and slightly convex as if they had bubbled in the baking, and the effect was a lustrous, copper-coloured eiderdown. In a few places a tile had cracked, from something dropped or from the pressure of heavy furniture, giving more of a patchwork impression than ever.

Gioconda laughed and, with her hand on the doorpost, skidded past me into the hallway, the air of mute stoicism now unimaginable in her. She stood at the front door swinging her hat by its brim as I put my keys in my handbag and switched off a light or two. "Such a risk to say, 'What would I do without you,' but I offer you the words all the same, Jenny." When I opened the door she flapped her hat with a silencing motion at the thudding of drums that came down from the kraal of the nightclub on the hillside. "If, as Gianni says, only an unworthy friend tells troubles, then I am the most unworthy friend you ever had."

Again the incongruity of words and bearing — as she stepped out over my threshold lightly, proudly, proclaiming herself *"l'amica più indegna che tu abbia mai avuto."*

"I do nothing for you. I wish I could." I slammed the door behind us. "Why a risk?"

"Why, the evil eye, my dear. It's the sort of thing that gets said before . . ." As we went down into the dark tunnel, Gioconda made the gesture of exorcism.

"And the evil eye," I asked of her white shape as it drew ahead of me along the corridor. "Does that exist for you?"

She tilted her head as if she were truly considering, and then we were in darkness until I pressed the next button. "You know what Croce said about it."

"Of course I don't."

"That it doesn't exist. And that it is a most terrible thing."

When Gianni came back from Tripoli, Gioconda gave a party. At her house from time to time I had met those friends of hers — the relative who lived near Sorrento, the plump twin sisters, and two or three couples, youngish, quietish, who dropped in to leave a message or borrow a book. One could not say that her life was solitary; yet it lacked any current of companionship, other than Gianni's.

Once, in talking to Justin about Gioconda, I spoke of this absence, in her life, of close attachments, blaming Gianni for draining away from her the time and impetus to make the very associations that would have freed her from him. I said, "She should be meeting others."

"Granted," said Justin, "that he's the prize bounder of all time, just as you say — a howling cad. Still, consider a little the life here of such a woman, if she's as you describe her." Justin always put in phrases like "if she's all you say" or "according to you," to indicate to me that I was over-enthusiastic about Gioconda, the victim of a schoolgirl crush. "A city like this — that has never had a middle class till now, and now that they do exist the middle class are precisely the people who wish to preserve the myth of their own non-existence and perpetuate the gulf between rich and poor. Assuming she needs a little human society — this friend of yours is free to choose companions from bigots, fascists, provincials, reactionaries of all kinds: rich foreigners playing at living in Italy; or portly youths calling themselves Marchese and displaying on the mantelshelf in July the Christmas card signed 'Umberto.' She can hearken indefinitely to matrons on the subject of silverware and pelmets, and in the evenings she can go out to play bridge and hear the local scandal about someone who spoke in favour of divorce . . . If you and I are refugees from the nit-picking and name-dropping of our native land, think what the comparable tuft-hunting circles must be round here. The fact is that life as a permanent fixture of a town like this can be a pretty lonely business. And you are the best thing that's happened to La Gioconda in years."

Justin liked to be sceptical about Gioconda, and after a while I stopped talking to him about her, for I felt that my admiration generated antagonism in him. Now and then, when Justin and I discussed our war wounds, compared our respective theatres of service, I would think that he might have this bond, at least — the horrors of war — in common with Gioconda, and was tempted to bring them together in something of the way that old campaigners are got together at a regimental dinner. Ultimately, however, it had pleased me to know them separately. Yet it was odd that they had never met, not even by chance. Several times Gioconda asked me to bring Justin to dinner or to tea, or on some drive we were taking, but at first these invitations coincided with Justin's trips or appointments; and later I did not even relay them to him, for I felt that he was prejudiced against her.

In other matters, too, Justin made a habit of pitting reason against my enthusiasms, somewhat after the fashion of Serafina. Though he urged me to remain artless, he would invariably point out flaws in my spontaneous judgments; it made him feel sound, judicious. I too wished to be governed by reason — to a reasonable extent — but not to be used as a foil for someone else's rationality. One cannot wish to be a sort of flint off which reasonable observations are struck like matches.

"Of course you'll bring him," Gioconda said, when she told me of the party she was giving, and I agreed of course I would. I did ask Justin if he would come, but he was flying to Rome that same day for the opening of an international conference on fisheries. "We're fated, he and I," said Gioconda, when I told her. But she went on, "Perhaps it's for the best. You don't want to give all your time to one. You should be meeting others."

Gioconda hung lanterns from the pergola at one end of her terrace, and at the other end she installed a group of musicians — two youths and a dark, lovely girl — whom she had hired for the evening. Inside, her study was almost untouched, but the *salotto* had been rearranged to allow for a long table where the supper was served — "a lavish supper," as I shamelessly described it to Norah in a letter, with so many dishes of rice and lobster and chicken, of shrimp and octopus, eggplant and squash, and above all of sweets: *zuppa inglese* in a white dish, tiny cakes sugared in green or pink; and ices in the form of fruits delivered that afternoon by Caflisch in a tub of dry ice, each with its strong or delicate colouring, its bloom of frost that dissolved to a gloss as soon as the platter was set on the table.

The women were all like that — like smooth, cool

fruit — that evening. Dresses then were full-skirted and came below the knee, but the impression was all of lightly drawn forms and clear colours. I remember the shining hair, drawn back, or falling forward over summer-coloured skin, the slender shoulders and wrists, and slim brown legs; and the cat crouching rodent-like under a sofa, fiercely watching. Of the men, all were personable, confident, in the way of Italian men; each one interesting to himself. None was of Gianni's age, though none was very young. Several couples — the majority perhaps — were married; but the atmosphere was one of courtship.

Gioconda, a little nervous, came among us in a dress the colour of poppies, with a narrow crimson ribbon threading the coils of her hair. The summer night, the house, the antiquated music, all increased the untopicality that attended the events of Naples — the sense that this might be any year, any era, and that only the season was essential.

One particular thing remains with me of that evening. Late, we went outside to dance. The terrace was cleared of its usual furniture, but along the sides a few low tables and rattan chairs had been set. The orchestra, which until then had played "airs" — the music of old songs, most of them Neapolitan — as a background to our talking and eating, changed character. The beautiful girl with the guitar had been to Brazil, it turned out, and had brought back music to dance to; and over Gioconda's terrace the couples circled and parted, then drew together, sprang forward or retreated, with steps of such calculated vitality, such urgent hesitation, that the wild music seemed at times almost formal and part of some ritual long-determined, much rehearsed.

What I particularly remember is this. Many of the women had taken off their sandals, kicking them away to the edge of the terrace, and were dancing on bare brown feet — this and the savage reverberations of the music contrasting violently with the smooth lips and elegant dresses, arched eyebrows and immaculate hair. As we danced, a glass was swept from one of the little tables, by the swirl of a skirt or a shawl, and smashed on the tiles, the fragments going everywhere, indistinguishable from the coloured tessellations. No one stopped. No one even looked down. The dancers spun back and forth under the lanterns and the bare feet went flying in and out among the spikes of glass. It was only when the musicians paused that Tosca came out with a brush and swept the pieces away. I don't think that anyone was hurt; yet the incident, with its sensation, though unexperienced, of glass biting through flesh, in retrospect dominates that party of Gioconda's; and the memory is tinged with horror.

# ❧ XI ❧

ONE LAST TIME we met by chance, Justin and I, on a hot Saturday afternoon of July, when I was on my way up Via Duomo. Justin was coming down, on foot, but he turned back to walk with me. And I was going to see Gioconda.

"I've been in a museum. This place here." He took my arm, but released it because of the heat. "Armaments and porcelain, the bull-and-china shop. Dreary, as a matter of fact — everything good was lost in the war or has gone somewhere else. Even the palazzo is a reconstruction." In passing he thumped his fist on the cliff of rusticated stone, as if to expose its essential flimsiness.

We strolled up the hot street, he in no hurry because he was at a loose end, morose, and glad to have run into me; I hanging back because I was undecided whether or not to take him with me to see Gioconda. We passed shop after little shop of wedding dresses, the mannequins with their over-optimistic post-war faces and their bodies tautly glazed in cheap satin, stiffly winged with tulle, attended by trappings for bridesmaids, mountainous hats for mothers-in-law.

Justin was enchanted with the windows. "This is a plot. You lured me here." He began to sing —

> *"Why am I always the bridesmaid,*
> *Never the blushing bride?*
> *Ding, dong, wedding bells*
> *Only ring for other girls —"*

getting approval from the passers-by. "Jenny me dear," he said, "let's buy you an outfit and marry you off. But to whom?"

"Look," I said.

"Always ordering me to look or listen. Influence of the Italian language — '*Guarda*,' '*Senti*' — assuming you'd address me familiarly, which is doubtful."

"Look. Listen. Come with me. I'm turning in here, at San Biagio."

"Oh. Your friend." He looked into another wedding window. "These shops — it's all like a photograph by Man Ray."

Now that he hesitated, I pressed him. "Come on."

"All right," he said, and we entered San Biagio dei Librai. "But I preferred her as a legend."

It went as badly as it was bound to do. I was too anxious that they should get on with one another, I

wanted them to show to advantage for my sake. But
Gioconda was having one of her untidy days, with her
hair straggling down uncombed; she was wearing an un-
becoming striped dress, and sandals with broken straps.
She lit cigarette after cigarette, narrowing her eyes
against the smoke in a fiendish grimace I had never seen
before. Justin was colourless, incurious, monosyllabic —
the very picture of scepticism fully confirmed. I wanted
to prompt them, to say to her, "Go on, be beautiful, be
original, as I described you," or to him, "Be witty, be
charming," as they sat being disobligingly dull. The
apartment had never looked so decrepit to me, and as
Justin's eyes passed over threadbare rugs and cushions,
and rested on the water-colour of Prócida in 1902, everything temporarily lost colour and character, even Gaetano's marguerites. When at last we came out of the
palazzo and set off in the direction of the Gesù Nuovo,
the street itself seemed excruciatingly squalid, and nothing more.

"Oh my God," said Justin, glancing into a soiled
courtyard.

I told him, "It's not all neglect. Some of it's the war,
still. The bombardment."

He smiled. "Naples *always* looks as if it had just been
under bombardment."

We walked on, not speaking, just as on the winter
evening when we had gone together to San Gregorio
Armeno; and I thought how little these passing months

had added to our intimacy. It was as if we had known
each other since childhood and had nothing left to disclose. Carried along in the early evening crowd, or
pushing our way against it, we reached an opening in the
street, near the church of Sant'Angelo a Nilo, where
there was, opposite the monument to the Alexandrians, a
stand that sold cool drinks. The stand, like a thousand
others in Naples, was decorated with swags of immense
lemons and oranges, and with the tapering fronds of their
leaves. On its counter, crescents of coconut floated in
bowls of water, and around its base stood classical
amphorae of terra cotta, some of them unmarked, some
of them inscribed with serpentine designs in red or
black — amphorae that in the past carried miraculous,
iron-bearing *"acqua ferrata,"* and now hold mere water
for the drinks pressed from the overhanging fruit.

"Jenny." Justin took my hand and led me across in
front of a fast car. "Have some lemonade." We leant on
the counter. "Why all these amphorae, I wonder? Why
not a tank of some kind?" He asked the plump girl who
was squeezing the lemons, and she told him, There's
nothing like it, the way it keeps the water cool.

She said, "We call them *'e'mmummarelle.'* "

"Think of that," said Justin to me. "Reflect a little,
Jenny, on the origins of such a word."

The girl was rosy, dressed in pink — immaculate, she
appeared to me, after slatternly Gioconda — and her
arm, as it rose lightly up and moved powerfully down to

crush the fruit on the small machine she used, was itself like some fascinating piece of equipment, smooth, un-erring, its manipulations perfectly meshed: something that might have won an award for functional design.

"A woman like that," said Justin.

I looked back from the girl to him.

He set down his glass. "I'm saying — a woman like that. Superb, phenomenal."

"I'm sorry?"

"Your friend, I'm saying. Gioconda."

It's annoying, when you are putting things together in this way and have made them fit, to come upon a piece or two you can't accommodate. For instance, I recall now that Gianni and Justin actually met — they did meet once, for a few minutes, a week or two after that, when Justin and I called one evening on Gioconda.

As we were leaving, Gianni came in. I had not seen him since the night of Gioconda's party. He was sun-tanned and looking well — looking fit, the expression would be, athletic and resilient. He was in a good mood, too — I remember dreading that he would talk his inane English to Justin, or come out with jokes about kilts and sporrans; I was apprehensive of Justin's opinion of him, once more as if I were responsible. Instead it went well — the very reverse of the uneasy afternoon when I introduced Justin and Gioconda. They were civil with one another, and even exchanged some marine observations connected with Gianni's fishing expeditions off Libya. It turned out, too, that Justin had spent some weeks of war in a part of Africa once familiar to Gianni.

"There were three white men there in my time," Gianni declared. "Three only. A German, a Dane, and me. We spoke Swahili with one another."

What a lie, thought I.

Justin, laughing, came out with some throaty words, and added in English, "It's all I remember — all I ever knew, in fact." Gianni at once responded with what must, from his attitude, have been some little speech of compliments or greeting. And I felt, at this unexpected, authentic accomplishment, the same unwilling astonishment I had felt on first seeing Gianni's apartment in Rome.

Nothing more than that. They shook hands, and parted. It is only the fact that they met that surprises, cropping out in retrospect. It is one of those little dependencies of memory that suddenly demand self-government. One is unreasonably angered with such a fact for existing, for making one wonder, as it does, what else has been forgotten. It spoils everything, and ought to be abolished. Was there not a follower of Pythagoras who was put to death because he pointed out an unaccountable flaw in the mathematical theory of universal harmony?

Another missing item is the report — the one I was at work on all this time. The report is missing not for any reason that alarms or touches me, however, but because it is not interesting enough to mention. The seasons I have described, the moods and incidents that shaded or illumined our four lives, occupied a tiny fraction, only, of the many hours and days given over to my work on that report — hours and days during which I, along with others, converted sheaves and rolls and heavy piles of paper from a foreign language into a form of English that was in its way more alien to us. Yet, while I know exactly where, in Via Calabritto, I bought a pink silk shirt I sometimes wore to work, or can recall at will the jingle chanted by my *portiere*'s child when he brought me my letters, not a phrase of that report comes back to me, not a single fragment of the sections and subsections and indented appendices on which, with technical dictionaries spread open under paperweights and annotated pages overflowing on to window-sills and chairs, I expended the greater part of my energies and days.

The importance of our work was constantly brought home to us. That was one reason why we doubted it. But mainly it was the level of its presentation — in the narrowest, the most belligerent context — that repelled our confidence; and the pathos of our superiors, their self-laudatory defending of the world from perils into which just such mentalities as theirs had plunged it. Lacking human reference, they reduced the most imperative matters to boredom: they might kill us, but they could never engage our interest.

That summer the city was less of a daily distraction than it had been at the start, for I had come to accept its apartness and its continuity — in the way that, in the course of a frightening dream, one comforts oneself, without waking, with the knowledge of reality and the certainty of returning to it. Because of this I could be, in the office, more as they wished me to be; never speaking now of the city or of my life in it, except to grumble companionably once in a while about a dishonest taxi-driver or a disastrous dry-cleaner; standing drinks at the Officers' Club on the Queen's Birthday and helping decorate the corridor for the Fourth of July. As a show of good faith one might work up indignation over a telephone breakdown, or because some folder of statistics arrived with a page missing. It was by the signs of dissatisfaction that we were bound together.

When our mission first came to Naples there had been continual talk about the necessity of adjusting to the area — the word adjusting reiterated as if we were nothing more than a set of short-wave radios that could, with a bit of fiddling, be tuned in to foreign programmes. The desirability of bearing up, or at least of not breaking down, had been impressed on us. It had never for a moment been intended that we should come to like the place.

It was at Bagnoli that I discovered the inertia of military men. As it was the habit of those warriors to deride as ineffectual the pleasures of the mind, a dynamism was implied in the conduct of their own unspeculative lives. Yet I would pass them, those men of action, huddled over milk shakes in the American restaurant in Santa Lucia as I set out for Spaccanápoli, or would see them gloomily slumped there at the bar on my return from an expedition to the islands. The pastel girls might take a bus to Amalfi or Ravello, Germani would escort his children into the crater of Vesuvius, "for an outing" as he said, but the timid activists seldom ventured far from the base. They spoke of food, and of losing weight; some took photographs, some followed the stock market. Their clubs, their PX, and a flat in a streamlined building within striking distance of these — that was, ideally, the pattern of the life of adventure: supine, incurious, complaining, they awaited the command that would animate them.

There were exceptions — which were made, if mild, the subject of taunts; and, if pronounced, the subject of a dossier.

Even the locally recruited clerks and couriers preferred, I think, the unexceptional, rather than have confusing elements in so consistent an establishment. By that summer I had given up using their real names of Gennaro or Carlo or Luigi, and was calling them Gerry and Louie and Charley just as everyone else did, and making them presents of cartons of Lucky Strikes bought at the PX for the purpose.

"You must do something very secret out there," Gioconda remarked once, and Gianni agreed, "God knows what she's up to. She never says a word about it."

"If you knew," I told them. "If you only knew how boring it is." It was again the contrast between their lives and mine. They, who spent their days freely using their intelligence, could never conceive of work such as mine. "You couldn't even imagine it."

Gianni groaned. "God almighty, when I think what I was doing at your age."

And Gioconda said, "Will she never understand?"

Of all the Mezzogiorno, only the report did not recognise the summer that year. As July came to a close, everything else slackened and changed. Those who could leave the city did so — the hot, dry, dirty streets were inhabited now only by the poor. The poor took the city over, appearing in big families or small battalions on Via Caracciolo or in Piazza dei Martiri — places where in winter they seldom showed themselves, or came as single spies. Along the seafront, any polluted point of access was alive with bathers, and a horde of near-naked children flapped and thrashed around the walls of Lucullus's castle.

The heart of the city became an interior, a dark centre of discomfort. Progress, in ripping out tracts of vineyard or vegetable garden, had only sealed that congested labyrinth more completely with concrete and bitumen, only made it the more unfit to bear its breathless summer. A portion of Spaccanápoli was still spoken of, without irony, as "the Gardens of San Gennaro," though street was laid on street there, and house on house, as if they had been tangled together in an earthquake.

Still they had their seasons, the pavements of Naples, those square stones of Via Tribunali or San Biagio dei Librai. In winter, *nespole* ripened there, pale spheres like unyielding apricots; in summer figs, green or magenta; and later there would be walnuts and lavender, and the fruit of the cactus. Heaped in cartons or baskets, spread on newspaper or simply on the ground, they burgeoned alongside piles of second-hand clothes and underclothes, beside mounds of threadbare blouses and discoloured corsets and all the other doubtful merchandise that bloomed there perennially.

Near Gioconda's house, in summer, a man in a wheelchair used to sell goldfish, which were displayed swimming about in a blue plastic baby-bath. And once in a while near the Porta Capuana, I would come across a salesman of ordinary sparrows, fifty lire each, squatting on the steps of Santa Caterina and passionately calling attention to the fluttering contents of his wicker cage.

Gioconda was away a lot, spending the weekdays in the islands when the crowds were less. She made arrangements to visit her sister at Nice, then postponed them. "I can't face travelling at this time of year. At least not till after Ferragosto. At Nice, too, it's frightful — crowds, you can imagine. Even Luciana writes me that I should wait." The truth was that she was unwilling to go so far from Gianni, and that she disliked leaving home. When I asked her what she would do in the summer, if she could freely choose, she laughed. "Perhaps in our old age, who knows, Gianni and I will be able to take trips to Assisi or Viareggio — *come le coppie cafoni.*"

Gianni himself had been in Zurich on business, and at Venice; had spent a fortnight at Portofino with his children. Returning, he had an accident — not a serious one, though he hurt his head and his knee, but the car was towed to a garage at Genoa and would be out of commission for a couple of months.

"It must be a wreck, then," I exclaimed, when Gioconda told me.

"Not at all. It's August — that's the thing. Nobody works, nothing can be done."

Some days later, arriving at Naples in a rented car, Gianni joined Gioconda on Capri.

Justin was to fly to Gibraltar at the end of the summer, and go on to Spain. From there he might go home to see his parents. In the autumn, he said, he would be back at Naples to finish his work with the Aquarium. I wondered whether, once away, he would return so soon, or ever.

It pleased me to hear their plans, to think of them all going in different directions. It made me feel stable, settled, at peace, at home; in a place, for the first time, that was not a preparation for another setting or a wider experience, and which I had no wish or reason to leave. I was immune to the mid-August holiday and its shifting guises of calamity and release; and to the endless repetition, "Before Ferragosto," "After Ferragosto" . . .

Only the report went on accreting, piling up, it seemed, more pages than we produced, being carried away in teetering loaves to be mimeographed into innumerable copies all marked TOP SECRET. When we had dealt with displacement and dredging and docking, there was refuelling and provisioning and logistics, and when those had been cleared up there was always security to fall back on, for there was never enough of that.

The Colonel, who had got hold of a small sailing boat and a Swedish girl friend, was genial these days and even went so far as to praise my industry, remarking that I seemed to be getting adjusted to Naples at last.

Just before Ferragosto I fell ill. That morning Serafina went up to the street in my place and told the Colonel to go on to Bagnoli by himself. Finding Justin there with his car, she delivered the message to them both. During his solitary drive the Colonel must have reflected on the coincidence of my illness with the approaching holiday, for he telephoned from the office to say that he was sending Germani back with the car to take me to the doctor. Although it meant getting dressed and making a winding journey up to the American Naval Hospital behind Naples, I was feeling sick enough to be glad of going there. A young officer took my temperature and diagnosed the Asian flu.

"What's your superior's name?"

I had learnt to recognise the Colonel in this description. From his office the doctor telephoned the Colonel and told him I must stay in bed until after the holidays. The Colonel having planted the seed of deception, I felt as grateful to this young man as if I had been malingering and he had abetted me. Even Germani, helping me back into the car, assured me I didn't look well, as if there were some doubt about the validity of my case.

On the descent from Via Manzoni towards the Posillipo, we came in full sight of the gulf of Naples. That high, open part of the city, the top tier of its arena, is a suburb, now, of identical modern blocks in pastel colours; hypocrite officialdom, seeking to minimise its guilt by implicating others, has named for the poets the avenues that spawn these parti-coloured cubes ("Like all those Piazza Mussolinis," Gioconda used to say, "that became Piazza Matteottis overnight, and could change back some other night just as fast; convenient, even to the number of letters"). But then it was still a countryside that looked to Naples on the one hand, and on the other across Pozzuoli to Cape Misenum.

It was a fierce day, clear, hotly coloured, every rise and declivity of the city dryly distinct. Slums, fields, churches, mountains and sea unfurled themselves around the volcano as on the plan of some extravagant place that could exist only in fancy. Germani drove more and more slowly, he leaning forward in his seat and I in mine as if we expected some climax to this great scene, might see it seized by some vast convulsion.

We came down to the shore at Mergellina, into streets already decorated for the festival of Piedigrotta, lankly strung with coloured bulbs as separate as ill-strung beads, melancholy in the midday sun. A hundred summer cafés had flowered around the tiny port, and stalls decorated with shells were selling oysters and mussels and the mossy, shapeless seafood called *"carnúmmola."* Red and purple, strung with floats of cork, the nets were spread there across the footpath and the road and, over it all, the children scrambled and darted with no sign of belonging, except to the city itself.

At home, Justin called me. I told him, "I'm ghastly sick. They say it's Asian flu." I told him about going to the hospital. "I really do feel seedy."

"Shall I come? Can I do something?"

"Thanks, no, absolutely nothing. I'm going to sleep. But I won't be able to come tomorrow." It was an appointment we had, to go to a concert in the amphitheatre at Pompeii.

"Oh — the concert, that's nothing. I'll give the tickets to somebody or other. Only sorry you're feeling seeders."

"No, don't be silly. Of course you should go . . . Take someone else."

"For instance?"

"Well — I don't know — there must be someone. A female colleague."

"They're all married. Or unmarried."

"Someone from Bagnoli, then." I was like a mother urging an unsociable child.

"Your friend," he said. "Shall I ask your friend?"

"My . . . ? Well of course. A good idea."

"I'm only joking."

"But of course you could call her. Just the job."

"You think so? Just the job? Won't Don Giovanni put his stiletto in my back?"

"Certainly. But be fearless."

"Bloody, bold and resolute. That's me." We were silent, then he laughed.

"What are you laughing at?"

"At the bare idea. Do you think that expression means bare in the sense of mere, or that the idea is being exposed to us, naked and undisguised?"

"Goodbye," I said.

"Look, I will come over this evening. See how you are. About seven, say."

I asked him, "Are you trying to redress the balance?"

"No. I am redressing the bare idea."

Justin came that evening to see me, and stayed for an hour or so. He made a jug of orange juice, and we sat in the living-room and drank it in the half-light because it was still too hot to open the shutters. Gioconda's name was not mentioned between us — then, or ever again.

Gioconda herself came to visit me a few days later. By then the holiday had passed. The city, as she told me, was empty; while the sea, as I saw, was teeming with life. I had got up for her visit, and she begged me to go back to bed.

"It's too hot," I told her. "Because I had to raise the shutters. I can't lie all day in a dark room."

She remarked, "I suppose in America we would have air conditioning."

"In Africa we had ceiling fans." It was the first time we had talked about the weather with one another. I turned my head to say this to her, but found her staring at me. "What's the matter?"

"You look so sick. You told me it was only the flu."

"So it is. There's an epidemic. I'll be better in a few days."

"In a few days I'll be gone, to Nice. It's all arranged . . . Look after yourself then, while I'm away."

"So you're really going?"

"Yes, I must. It's time. I'll be back soon — three weeks or so."

I wondered about Gianni, whether he would visit her there, whether he had come to Naples over the holiday; but for once she had not mentioned him. When she got up to go I put my hand on her arm, and said, "How different from when you were leaving Naples last time, for Tripoli." But the recollection hurt her, for she covered my hand with hers and did not smile, and I was sorry to have spoken of it. She leant forward to embrace me, but I told her, "Keep away," and she drew back instantly. "I don't want you to come down with anything."

After she had gone I realised I had been expecting Justin, who sometimes came by at that time of day, and was glad that he had not come — because, illogically, I grudged the impression that Gioconda had made on him after all. But when he did arrive, late and in a hurry, then perversely I wished I might have seen them together; as it would not be the same another time, afterwards, when the summer was over.

When I was discovered to have hepatitis, even the Colonel came to see me. It was the only time he ever came to my flat, and Serafina was proud of my having him there and completely taken in by his moustache and by the campaign ribbons pinned to his summer uniform. I remember nothing of what I said to him, being by that time very ill and forgetful of his existence, let alone his presence; but I do recall that he urged me not to worry about the report, which he felt must be on my mind.

Serafina impressed him, too, and because of that I was not made to go to hospital as everybody wished, but remained at home throughout the confused weeks that followed.

When, after Ferragosto, I had got no better, Germani had driven me again to the hospital, and brought me home re-diagnosed as a serious case. There was no one now for me to pass on this news to, other than the Colonel — for that morning Justin had flown to Spain in a plane belonging to the United States Navy. I did write a calm note to Norah telling her I had jaundice, and she wrote hysterically back saying I must be very careful and that this was prevalent in Italy. She and Edmund had tried to ring me up, but the telephone system of Naples was one too many for them.

In fact the telephone seldom rang during those weeks, except for enquiries that came from the office. Even in the worst of the illness I would think of Bagnoli and the PX and the report and the Colonel, and be glad to be free of them and at home, nauseated, feverish, and turning deep yellow. When you are ill you can only be yourself — whereas in an office one is required always to be somewhat false, at least when one is subordinate. The preference for a serious disease over office life struck me, even at the time. Mostly my thoughts were not so coherent, and once or twice visited by passages of delirium.

In the jumble of those indistinguishable nights and days, two things grotesquely predominated. One was the festival of Piedigrotta, whose songs surged into my rooms from Mergellina and from every radio on the Posillipo. All night the celebrations flared red and green around my walls in fireworks and floodlighting, recreating an active volcano at the other — the wrong — end of the harbour; in the day, causing foreign contestants (for no Neapolitan would have contemplated so useless an expenditure of energy, and the race was always won by a Dane or a New Zealander) to swim out to Capri, and skiffs to tack back and forth around a series of buoys. The festival was of the same official duration as the active period of my illness: it reached its own climax, and entered its own decline.

The other thing was an ineradicable scent, exotic, sickening, which had somehow got into my rooms, I do not know from where. Until I was quite recovered I was always conscious of that sweet smell, and never found out where it came from, how it had infiltrated the mind, perhaps, or the imagination, rather than the nostrils. Perhaps it lingered from some tuberoses Justin once brought me; or from the perfume, with one of those names — Sin, or Scandal, or Woman — that Gioconda always wore.

# ❧ XII ❧

GIOCONDA GONE, Justin in Spain, I had no visitors. The few casual acquaintances who might have come were off to islands or mountains. Each morning Serafina let herself in, and that was the only interruption in identical days that I passed in bed or, when the disease began to ebb, out on the terrace. The mere fact of growing less ill, the privacy and silence of those high rooms, the emancipation from bureaucracy, brought pleasure of a kind I had never known; pleasure that was far from negative, though it owed so much to lack; that, in looking inward rather than ahead, signified, I suppose, the end not even of youth but of childhood.

Below the windows there was always something going on. In the earliest morning there were boats below, on a sea at that hour indistinguishable from inflamed sky; one lone boat, or a pair, or a group of them drawing up nets or lobster pots. No sound ever came landward from these boats except sounds of the sea — soft plashings of their work, or the mild collisions of hull and tide. If the fishermen spoke to one another, it was in voices too low to reach the shore. The men, like the boats, were weathered, single-purposed, uncolourful. In each of their practised movements there was the intentness, the restraint, that suggest not an industry but an existence.

They were always there. Throughout the day, when the water near the rocks was logged with swimmers and with rafts and sailing boats, there on the periphery would be one of these boats, a wedge of grey or brown in that kaleidoscope, a fly in all that ointment. In the evening they were to be seen rocking on the wash of a pleasure-launch or in the wake of the fast white ferry bound for Ischia. In the night, no matter what hour one looked for them, they were out with acetylene lamps and you could see the single figure standing in the stern with the oars, and the other kneeling at the prow and bending into a circle of clear green light.

At first during that convalescence I could do nothing but watch. Walking from one room to the next was exhausting, a few pages of a magazine or a book brought tears of fatigue. Sometimes I slept right through the morning and woke to find a tray on the bedside table and Serafina gone. But nothing intruded on my new pleasure; all this time was mine.

One morning it rained. Waking late I found the room dim, and the bathers' screams suspended. The gulf was grey with rain that fell steadily, discreetly, without thunder. There was no wind, but for the first time in months the passage of air could be felt about the room. I pulled up a chair and sat at the terrace doors in an immense relief: I'd had no idea how much I had missed the rain. The hills, the buildings, the boats looked refreshed and grateful. The sea itself seemed to be thirsty.

I greeted Serafina with "The rain!" as if it were a development that vitally affected both of us. She at once reproved me, it was a sprinkling only: "*Sghizzichea.*" And over the breakfast dishes she loudly sang a tragic song, "How it rains. *Ggiesù,* how it rains."

The next day was fair again, the bathers were back. But the break was there, you felt it. We had got to the end of summer and there had been a change. I began to sleep less and to be interested in food. Germani drove me up to the hospital two or three times for blood tests in which a dye was injected into my vein to illuminate the declining course of the disease. I had a letter from my brother; and a Get Well card signed by all the office — the local staff having inscribed their names dutifully at the bottom, surname first, one neatly under the other like a petition. With an eye to conditions at Naples, the PX must have stocked up heavily with Get Well cards, for any number of these, each one different, ultimately reached me.

The first Saturday after the rain everybody was out using up what now remained of the good weather. Some were there at sunrise, lining the rocks like early risers getting first place for a spectacle. It was September, a ripe, flawless day. I was lying on the bed in a dressing-gown, reading. Serafina had said goodbye to me and gone to the door. I heard her talking to someone as she let herself out, and a man's voice said impatiently, "That's all right. Go, go." "No" was repeated two or three times, and the door closed loudly. And the same voice, the man's voice, said, "Jenny."

Strangely, I thought at first that it might be my brother standing there so unexpectedly, or even Justin, and I could not take in the fact of its being Gianni. I had not been thinking much about Gianni, and it took a second or two to get the idea of his being there. But it was Gianni — Gianni was standing in the doorway of my room with a sheaf of flowers, wrapped up, beneath his arm.

He himself looked bewildered, as if I had taken *him* by surprise. He had a light-coloured suit on and a blue shirt, and looked very well dressed, almost dandified. Then I saw it was all wrong, the way he looked and his turning up like that. And even before I absorbed that realisation, I had said, "What is it, what's happened?" One talks of being speechless with shock, but there are times when the comprehending words are uttered before the brain has formed their meaning. I remember thinking, The flowers are normal, to reassure myself: if there had been a calamity, a death, he wouldn't have stopped to get me flowers.

He was looking at me in that way, puzzled and alarmed. I raised myself against the pillows as he came across the room and stood beside the bed. He suddenly dropped his bunch of flowers — that is, he just moved his arm as if the flowers were not there, and they fell to the floor with a paper crash. At the same moment I put my book face-down on the sheets. This laying down of our weapons occurred as he seated himself on the edge of my bed — not greeting me or taking my hand, but trembling all over like a domestic animal that has seen something wild.

Awareness of a sick-room, of my condition, seemed to work on him vaguely and to introduce some echo of restraint over whatever it was he had to tell me. "You don't know," he said.

"Gianni, my God, what is it?"

"She's gone. Gioconda's gone to Spain."

"To Spain?"

"Gioconda's left me." But he gave, in stating this, no impression of delivering himself of what he had to say. He had information for *me*, I could see it. He hesitated again, and then he said, "She's with the Scotsman."

It was bizarre, his saying it like that, *"lo Scozzese"* — the comic name he had used for Justin, uttered in this context devoid of comedy. The knowledge was both physical and mental, like an electric shock. I could feel it entering my ears and breast and fingers, circulating in me.

"Do you understand me, Jenny?" Gianni's impulse to break the news gently was transfigured, as I stayed silent, into the need to urge the situation on me and obtain a response comparable to his own. "With your friend."

It came to me how Justin had said, "Your friend. Your friend Gioconda." To remind himself, possibly; to accuse himself — or Gioconda. I felt the same new, frightening surprise I had experienced on learning that I had a recognised, serious disease, not just a passing ailment that the system would absorb and forget within hours or days. I felt knowledge, as I say, coursing in my body, making everything different.

Gianni leant forward for a moment, his elbows on his knees, his hands over his eyes. I thought he must be weeping, but he looked up dry-eyed, as if he had merely been trying to concentrate on a complicated matter. He looked terrible, his face whitely disarrayed; one could not say that he suddenly looked like an old man, but you could see how he would be in age, the fullness turned to folds, the eyes more fixed. At the same time he looked better too, more like a real person.

I still had not spoken to him. I could hear his breathing, heavy and regular, like a patient in anaesthesia.

"Tosca told me. But there was a letter lying there too. It's been lying there ten days."

"What do you mean? Lying where?"

"San Biagio. She telephoned me, Gioconda, almost three weeks ago, and said she wasn't going to Nice. She asked me to come to Naples."

"You didn't come."

He shouted, "No." He controlled himself, laid his hands, now, on his knees to steady them, to steady himself. "I came only this morning. I've come this moment from San Biagio. I thought she would still be there."

So there had been a calamity after all. The flowers were for Gioconda.

"You hadn't been in touch with her?" He shook his head. "You were punishing her," I said, punishing him.

"We had a quarrel." Gianni made a pronouncement of this, as if their relations had been otherwise unclouded. "Over my life in Rome. Over a woman." We were quiet again until he repeated, "Her letter has been there all this time, right there on the table in the hall." This fact of the letter lying there like an undetonated explosive was the last straw for him. I knew what he felt: to me too the tranquillity of my convalescence now appeared to have taken place in grotesque ignorance of this. "You can read it. It says nothing — I mean, nothing more. She mentions you. She says she hasn't been able to write it to you — but I thought at first you might have known. From him."

I took Gioconda's note from him and read it. They may be married by now, I thought, handing it back.

Gianni folded it and put it into his wallet, carefully, as though conserving a piece of evidence. He put the wallet back into his trouser pocket, stretching out his leg to do so, his foot grazing the paper cone that contained the flowers. He said to me, "I am in agony" — the statement as blatant, as naïve as the caption of a silent film. He got up distractedly and walked round the bed. Coming back and standing beside me he put his palm against his breast. "A blow. Just what people say — I've had a blow. That's how it feels. As if I'd been struck by force."

He turned away once more and walked over to the terrace doors and stood there, a violet shape against the light. I heard the shuddering sounds of his tears.

It was appalling, this humbling of Gianni — as once before, when I had seen him plead with Gioconda and be refused; and compounded by the contrast with his accustomed facility for tears. I lay listening to him, so exquisitely aware of his grief that every detail on which my eye fell — the crease of a sheet, the fissure in a tile, the slight stain around the doorknob — commanded attention and became significant, as if my perceptions were trying to divert me out of self-preservation, in the way that one might offer trinkets to a frantic child.

I swung my legs down from the bed to go to him, but as I got to my feet he turned abruptly and was at my side again.

Gianni's sudden presence, and the effort of rising, affected my balance. Standing barefoot on the little rug by the bed, I swayed slightly and took a step aside. He put out his hand to steady me, grasping my arm above the elbow, his fingers completely circling the flesh through the cotton gown.

The contact recalled me to him — recalled me, that is,

as my self rather than as, simply, the recipient of his news — for he stared into my face with a shifting of sights, and again with the look of puzzlement and recognition.

"You're so thin, Jenny." Without changing its pressure, his hand on my arm acknowledged this, and his voice altered. "Almighty God, you're thin."

It is hard to convey, now, why it was touching, how touching it was, this involuntary solicitude of Gianni's. It was like the rain — I had not realised, until it fell, how deprived of it I had been, how greatly life had been lacking in this perfectly ordinary element. Tears — of weakness, loneliness, self-pity — rose to my own eyes. But most of all it was moving, this digression of Gianni's, by its show of a spontaneous human concern. The simple physical fact of Gianni taking hold of my arm and noticing how thin it had become gave us back for a moment our sense of existing outside of Gioconda's departure, and of being subject to human sensations other than suffering. Far from giving a sense of proportion, as it is said to do, disaster throws everything out of perspective: and this exchange of ours was hopelessly bound up with the disruption, the detail of my thinness merely thrown into relief by it — enhanced by it, in fact, like the cracked tile or the stain on the door.

Gianni still held my arm, and still I stood there with the backs of my legs touching the cool metal frame of the bed. We said nothing. The cries from the sea, which throughout this time had gone unheard, were all at once raucous and urgent, as if someone had unthinkingly turned up their volume. "So thin, Jenny," Gianni repeated, to pass the time, it might have been, while we entered into another stage of experience.

Without slackening his encircling fingers — as though my arm represented some source of meaning — Gianni embraced me, and I leant against him. His face, wet with tears shed for Gioconda, was lowered to mine. And when at last we lay down together, his hand, then releasing me, reached up from habit to the back of my head, to grope for the tortoise-shell comb he was accustomed to unclasping there.

Gianni and I sat by my windows in the dark, I in a deep chair with my legs beneath me, he on a stool alongside. My hand, over the chair-arm, rested, light, in his; comforted, serene, without suspense.

"She won't stay with him."

"That's it," said Gianni. "Tell me she'll come back. For it's all I can stand at the moment."

"She will," I obediently answered. As Gianni pointed out, it was necessary to get him through this day. "For him, it must be . . ."

"A grand passion."

"Yes. For her, it can only be —" I was going to say "despair"; but left it, again, unfinished. This time Gianni did not supply the word.

"Perhaps she has already left him."

"Perhaps."

Gianni said, "The poor bastard." Then, simply, "The bastard." He lit a cigarette and threw the match out over the terrace into the sea. When the cigarette was finished, he did the same with the end of it.

"Gianni," I said at length. "If Gioconda comes back, there'll be no use blaming her." It was my turn, now, to tell him things.

Gianni touched his head against my shoulder. "Sweet."

"It might even be that you would be different with her."

"What you mean is, it might be a lesson to me," said Gianni, but not smiling.

"It might make you kinder."

"Perhaps." Gianni looked doubtful. "The thing is, I don't think I could keep it up. It would be all right for a while, and then it would all be the same again. I don't know that I could change."

"On the contrary. I'm talking about your becoming more like yourself."

"That might be worse, in the end."

We were talking about him as we might have done behind his back.

"Besides, I have no desire to turn into one of those men you see about — reformed characters, you know; who have come to heel."

For a time we watched the lights lifting and sinking in

the water, the lights strung up the side of Vesuvius, the lighted curve of the town tapering away to darkness. Gianni moaned, thinking I suppose that Gioconda might not come back, and that if she did he might never see her. "Let me stay tonight." And he added ingenuously, "I ought not to be by myself."

I thought of how Gioconda had said to me, "Of course I could not bear it if, at the end of the day, it was you who were to go to bed with him."

I had put Gianni's flowers in a big glass vase, and they stood on a table near the windows, immense snapdragons, dozens of them, fierce and velvety, purple and orange and red. They had lain all afternoon on the bedroom floor.

"They'll revive," I said. "The flowers. Tomorrow they'll be fine." I began to dread tomorrow and how this might seem then. Finding Gianni there.

Gianni said, "They're Gioconda's favourite flower."

In this way it came about that on the following Saturday Gianni returned to Naples and did not go to San Biagio dei Librai.

# ☙ XIII ☙

"TODAY I WENT OUT, some few miles above Seville, to see the ruins of Italica. Do you remember I laughed, Jenny, at the idea of leaving Italy to visit Roman ruins — yet there I was walking a rough path among long dry grass, as grateful as any legionary for these familiar sights. *Civis Romanus sum*, it would appear. Because the walls are all down, and the site on high ground, there is an open, windswept atmosphere up there — difficult to imagine that the mosaic pavements were ever enclosed in houses or that the skyline was ever obscured by something more than the few cypresses that stand today. At the gate of the place, where one pays to enter, there was a poem inscribed that I thought you would have liked — a Spanish poet, and all I can remember is a reference to the weeds growing over the ruins like a public insult. In contrast with such astringency, such light and air, Herculaneum seems claustrophobic, a dense, decadent little enclave — too pleasurable, too ingrown. Too much like home.

"Otherwise — I have been in a great cathedral here in Seville, and walked under screens of vines in charming streets, visited the Alcazar. The avenues are lined with orange trees, the parks are still filled with flowers. It is all as mournful to me as if it were draped in black. Once I stopped at the edge of a garden to look at an inscription on a pretty house, thinking it perhaps another poem: instead it announced the headquarters of the Falange. Spain seems all like that — you never know whether it is to be poetry or horrors, or the two combined. Something evil is always turning up to remind me how things are, how I am.

"What I would like is — to come home. Instead, tomorrow, I am going to Madrid, then to Nice, at last, to Luciana. I will be back at Naples before the end of the year. If you can bring yourself to regard this as what it is — a low point in life, in my life — perhaps we shall meet . . . This evening I spend sitting here with the potted palms in a huge, glassed-over courtyard of the hotel — cold in spite of heating and in spite of a tumbler of Spanish scotch. There are two or three other people in a far corner who are whispering as if this were the cathedral itself, and the air of sobriety would be total were it not for a poor mad girl in beautiful clothes who sits talking to herself and occasionally gets up and wanders round the empty tables pulling the flowers out of their little vases as if she were rehearsing Ophelia. She is fair and quite lovely, though emaciated, and the most dreadful thing of all is the gravity with which the waiters answer her preposterous questions, conspiring against her with her infirmity. What else can they do? — but this alone would be enough to make one mad.

"When this is no longer bearable, I'll go and have dinner — in a vast restaurant off the courtyard, in which at this season only one or two tables are occupied though all are laid — then go upstairs. My room has a solemn luxury — dark wood, double doors with polished fittings, exquisite linen: being comfortable is not something taken lightly here. It is all wonderfully dated, yet wonderfully kept up to date, like one of those antiquated motor-cars that has never been bettered and is in perfect running order — you know the kind, when you lift up the bonnet the engine is immaculate, its caps and taps glittering, all bronze and brass . . . In fact this hotel seems to be expecting, even to merit, something better than human guests — as if it had been intended for some superior order of being. I feel it must regard us, poor crazed and muddled mortals trailing over its marble floors, as a public affront, like the weeds of Italica.

"Again — I would like to come home; and to have familiar things, things that would make me less unfamiliar to myself. Today the hairdresser told me that my hair is *'muy castigado'* from the summer teasing: I too am much punished from the summer teasing, and wish I were leaving for Naples, not for Nice . . ."

Years later I arrived one spring evening in Seville, not alone, and sat in the glass-domed courtyard of Gioconda's letter, among the ferns and palms. Watched over by a sombre waiter and one or two wintry guests, the two of us made up, from a dish of salted crackers formed in letters of the alphabet, love-words that we spread out on our little table. We had managed to compose an indecent phrase or two before the waiter's approach forced us to eat our words. Looking out our bedroom window before dawn we saw a group of cab-drivers in the street below warming themselves at a bonfire lighted on the pavement, while one of their number read to them from an out-stretched newspaper. The following morning we were told that the Pope had died.

Walking out in the city for the first time, we found it swathed in black, draped, wreathed, shuttered, depopulated: grotesquely adapted to the image of Gioconda in her sorrow walking these same streets, as if the city were, nightmarishly, living out one's private associations with it.

What stayed with me after reading Gioconda's letter was the completeness of Justin's disappearance from our lives. She asked nothing better than to take up her life as if he had never entered it; just as I wished now to go on, leaving him behind. Her chaotic flight had freed Gioconda from unnatural sacrifice; it had freed me from idealisation of her. Even Gianni, according to my reasoning, stood, in his grief, to regain himself. Only Justin remained unaccounted for, not a beneficiary under this distribution of spoils. He seemed fictitious, a sort of sub-plot, something that had no existence other than to aug-ment her experience and mine, to contribute to our legend. He himself had strengthened this impression by the defences — of language, of manner, of making love — he had constructed; had become their victim, like those heavily fortified towns that invite their own down-fall by suggesting that there is something within to be assaulted.

He had made himself appear, in retrospect, too easily elucidated — more so than Gianni, who was constantly exposing and betraying himself, and of whom there had yet remained something to discover.

Folding Gioconda's letter and putting it carefully back — as carefully as Gianni had done — into its envelope, I said aloud the name not mentioned in it: "Justin Tulloch." The words made no change, did nothing to bring him to life; unless by leaving, echoless, the sense of incompletion.

Justin, if I hoped to exorcise you by pronouncing your name that day, for the last time, I was unsuccessful. For no name has haunted me as yours has. Why — when a single properly directed enquiry would have provided the answer — have I looked for and failed to find your name ever since? — in telephone books, thin or weighty, from Brussels to Chicago; and once in Hollywood, balancing the flopping volume on my knee and turning pages while a voice droned on in the receiver about the creative impulse. Justin Tulloch — Tulloch, Justin; Tulloch, Justin P.; Tulloch, J. P. — it was your name that came to find me, after all, one day.

This summer — the summer, that is, of this year that has just passed — my husband, who is a lawyer, had business to do at Pinner. Pinner was once a pretty, village-like place, and not, as it has now become, a suburb of London. It was a Saturday late in August when, after weeks of icy rain, the weather had suddenly turned hot, brilliant and dry. While the business was being done, I walked through the town. The High Street (I suppose it was a High Street) ran down a short hill, and boasted, as the quite inappropriate saying goes, a number of tea-rooms. The one I turned into was, like all the tea-rooms of childhood, a combination of dun distemper and darker varnish. No arrow of that bright afternoon could pierce its leaded dark-grey panes, glassily dimpled as though by the impression of innumerable fingertips; or illumine the pinched lady — counterpart of a thousand others — who with a schoolroom gesture of her furled menu pointed out an empty chair at the end of the low, close room.

The place was hot with summer and humanity. In tea-rooms in England one must often share a table. Tea and cakes for the three other women at my table — there was not one man in that crowded place — had just been brought on a wooden tray. The ringleader of the three dispensed cups and saucers, forks and plates to her friends, reaching out in constricted gestures. She wore a sleeveless cotton dress printed with pink flowers, and her middle-aged, sunless white arms were too prominent — vulnerable and touching; she herself seemed conscious of the exposure as she repeatedly extended and withdrew them.

The waitress took my order, and I picked up from the floor by my chair somebody's discarded copy of that day's newspaper. By pushing the chair back a little against the mustard wall, I could open the paper in my lap.

Flowered woman set hand on flowered teapot. "Shall I be Mother?"

Cups, not matching, were extended. "Just as it comes."

I turned pages of the newspaper, in the total privacy of these few inches that were my inviolable claim on our table. We exchanged no looks, no words; unaffectedly they spoke, as if I were not there. I liked their ability to carry this off.

"I heard they went to Venice for the honeymoon."

"But only for a week."

When the tea came I managed to re-fold the newspaper, my elbows gouging my sides, and propped it between me and the table. It was placed so that the lower section of a page was visible. I helped myself to tea, and to a yellow cake that looked like a small segment pried out from the wall at my back, and I was able to read an item that came just below the crease of the page. It was a despatch from an island in the Caribbean.

### SEARCH DISCONTINUED FOR SEAPLANE

The search has been abandoned for a twin-engined amphibious plane overdue here since Thursday evening. The plane, which was returning from a scientific expedition to a nearby island, is presumed to have developed engine trouble in the last stage of its flight . . . In addition to a crew of three, the plane was carrying two unidentified passengers and a British scientist, Professor J. B. Tulloch from Edinburgh University . . . Professor Tulloch leaves a widow, Mrs. Lorna Staynes Tulloch of Elgin Crescent, Edinburgh, and two young sons.

"Another cuppa anyone?"

"Not me. In this heat."

"He has to have a dressing every day, like I was telling you. Well she said, I've got used to it now, you can get used to anything, but at first I can tell you my stomach turned over."

The cup in one hand, a forkful of cake in the other, I lowered my head over your name, Justin, at last, in that tearoom in Pinner, inches from the fair, greying topknots of my chattering companions. My stomach turned over, I can tell you, but one gets used to anything. The pang of irrational, posthumous jealousy, the shock of your alien new life that had already closed before I learnt of its existence; and your name I had sought everywhere. The middle initial, of which you were proud, was misprinted, there is always some irrelevancy of the kind. We had an appointment in Pinner, your name and I, and now I will never need to look for it again. The search has been abandoned.

Gianni raised himself on his elbow. The fold of the linen sheet stood up stiffly, whitely, around his shoulders, like the robe in a Bernini sculpture. "Now what's the news?"

"Several things," I said. "How do you know I have news?"

"Because you haven't asked me if I have any."

"I'll tell you when we've had something to eat."

In the wake of the disease I had developed gluttony, as if every organ were crying out for replenishment. As soon as Serafina washed up the lunch dishes and departed each afternoon, I would go into the kitchen and open tins, slosh soup into a saucepan, hack off slices of bread and cheese. During the previous night I had eaten up most of a cooked chicken and polished off a tin of Indian pudding from the PX. I stayed a little longer at Gianni's side, but all I could think about was food.

He followed me to the kitchen and stood in the doorway, thrusting his arms into his shirt. "What a lot of waste in tomatoes," he remarked, as if he had never seen them sliced before. He passed his hand up my neck, under my hair. "The yellow is fading."

"So I hope. I'd begun to think I was yellow for life."

"This illness of yours — it gives the thing a more macabre character than ever."

"I don't think I'm infectious any more."

Gianni groaned. "Oh lord, I hadn't even thought of that. No, I didn't mean that, though . . . It's like . . . It's slightly —"

"Necrophilous."

"Well — you're on the right track . . . Your toenails, even your toenails are yellow, Jenny."

I laid out strips of ham on a platter with one hand, and with the other put a folded slice into my mouth. Gianni watched me pile up a tray with bread and mozzarella, and fruit in a bowl of water. "Steady on," he said. "I'm not all that hungry."

"I am, though." I took two napkins from a drawer and stuffed them in the pocket of my dressing-gown.

"Another glass," said Gianni as I took up the tray.

"I'm not allowed wine." I had never been really sick before and enjoyed citing these prohibitions. "Or vinegar," I added — though even this could not move Gianni to carry a tray.

We sat on the terrace. It was another mellow, still

afternoon, and I stared at the city, at the mountains, at the sea, at the fluted palisades, far off, of Sorrento, enlarging my eyes to take them in. Impression, sensation, experience were famished too, and asking for replenishment: my eyes were as big as my stomach.

"Yes, you're looking better," Gianni said. He put the bottle of mineral water down in the shade beside his chair. "Now tell me. You've heard from her." I nodded, with my mouth full. "And I have not. Will I see the letter?"

"Could. But it isn't necessary." I wanted, most particularly, to keep it to myself, this final communication between Gioconda and me.

"Does she mention me?"

"Not in so many words."

"Gianni is only one word," he pointed out, to cover his disappointment.

I said, "She was alone when she wrote. By now she'll be at Nice with her sister."

Gianni tore off a frond from a bunch of grapes. I watched the fruit tremble in his fingers, as delicately as though it were still on the vine. "Is it over, then?" After a minute he got up and leant on the rail with his back to me, eating the grapes and tossing the seeds into the sea. At last he threw the stem away and came back and sat beside me. He took up my hand and laid it against his face and dropped it again.

"Gianni," I said. "In a word: Gianni. Go and fetch her."

Gianni put his bare foot up against the railing. "It could so easily go wrong, you see."

"It's what she wants." When he looked at me, I added, "Not that she says so."

"Well, there you are." But I could see that he would go. When he went on, "I'll have to get the car back," I thought of Gioconda getting a new dress for Tripoli, and wished the memory away. "How long will she stay there?"

"Till Christmas or so."

Gianni rocked himself back in his cane chair with his foot braced on the railing. Eventually he said, "You had something else to tell me. Several things, you said."

"Yes. They have asked me to go to America."

He and I stared at one another. *"O Dio."*

"I would have to be there in November. To present the report of this joint commission I'm with here. To submit the report, whatever that means." I saw myself walking up the steps of the Lincoln Memorial, which was the only building in Washington I knew the look of, an immense manuscript in my extended hands — something like the Presentation of the Virgin. "It's to do with last-minute changes, that sort of thing. I would have to sign on for at least another year."

"The last minute appears to be somewhat prolonged," Gianni observed. "How is the salary?"

"Low. But they will pay my fare, and I can go by ship."

"Will you be well enough?"

"By that time, yes."

"Do you know anyone there?"

"No. But I didn't know anyone here either."

"And now look at you." Gianni smiled, glancing up my bare legs to where my shoulder was coming out of the dressing-gown.

I laughed. I said, "I don't know why I'm crying. It's having been sick, I suppose."

Gianni shifted his chair beside mine. "It's terrifying," he said, reaching down to move the mineral water. "That's why." He took my right hand in his once more and I wiped my eyes with my left.

We sat still with our hands linked. I said, "We must look like Darby and Joan. Though I can't say I ever pictured them sitting beside the Bay of Naples."

"*Ma chi sono?*"

"Oh God, don't ask — they're a comfy old couple who sit by the fire."

"Well, since I am to be this comfy old John —"

"It's Joan, not —"

"— let me tell you my comfy old idea. I am going to telephone, now, to the shipping company and find out what ship you can take. I am not going to Gioconda until I see you settled, no matter what happens. I will put you on the ship." He released my hand and got up. "Quiet.

Quiet. Let me telephone, and afterwards we can talk about it. It would be better this way, it gives us more time."

I said, "I don't need more time."

"I meant — forgive me — for her and me."

He went in, and was back a second later. "Where's a pencil and paper?"

"In the —" I remembered Gioconda's letter in the drawer by the bed. "On the desk in the living-room."

I heard him on the telephone, using the precise, practised language that Italians have developed for making arrangements. I could see him reflected in the open glass door, lying back on my unmade bed, making ironic gestures of exasperation or enquiry with his free hand, which he then placed over the mouthpiece. "Which class?"

"First class," I called back. "They'll send me first class."

"Oh the good old taxpayer." In saying this he sounded quite like Justin. He sat up and started scribbling on the piece of paper. I could hear him repeating dates, rejecting them, getting others, reciting ports and prices. Finally he hung up and came back to me on the terrace.

"All right." He sat down and flattened the paper on his knee. "From Genoa, let's say, beginning of November. The others are too soon or too late." He reeled them off to me, each complete with its complications.

"Gianni, it's insane to go from here to Genoa. To go away from Naples in order to take a ship?"

"I will take you," he said. "I've been thinking about it. I will take you there, and I'll go on to Nice." He waited for me to speak, then continued. "It's a bit odd — it's extremely odd — but the whole thing's been odd. Unless that seems *too* odd to you."

I shook my head. I thought of Justin saying, "That is love. You must believe me, Jenny." Mainly I was struck by the luxury of having things taken out of my hands. I said again, "Genoa, though. When I'm here, at Naples."

"It's much better. Listen — leaving here, after all that has happened to you — you'll feel it less this way. Oh Jenny, a ship from Naples for America — have you ever seen that? These people, so sentimental that they cry when a train is going fifty kilometres, can you imagine? — oh God, all those cheap green trunks. Even if you could stand it, I couldn't." Tears of the old kind rushed to Gianni's eyes. "No, just take it from me. Genoa will be best. Unless you want to sail from England." I shook my head again. "What about your family? Don't they interest themselves in the form your life takes? Aren't they worried about you?"

"They worry about themselves. That is their thing, you see; what they do best."

"It's not really something that can be done well," Gianni said. "The other possibility would be — you could stay on here. They would give you something else to do, other work."

"Gianni," said I. "I will tell you something about my family." He thought we had disposed of my relatives, and his face recast itself for boredom. "Which will explain why I don't stay on here." I paused, at some mental intersection where many routes converged. "There was a time when I undertook to supply what was lacking in my brother's marriage. Though his wife did not know she was encouraging me to do this, it was something that, with a little thought, she might have known. Even after discovering it, there too I might have stayed on, shifting the position a little, doing the same thing differently, but for her intention to use me further — as a foil for her magnanimity. I was to be an object of forgiveness and understanding for the term of my natural life. Again, she did not know that she was doing this; again, she should have known it." Gianni made a face, as if this were asking for the moon. "I'm telling you this so you will know why I don't stay here and wait for Gioconda. Here too, some things have been the same. The difference is that I care about Gioconda, and could not bear the rest of our friendship to be a mutual demonstration of largeness of heart. It's too soon for us to be together again. What with one thing and another."

Gianni smiled. "Am I the one thing, or the other?" But he nodded. It was all obvious to him, and I think the only thing that baffled him was why anyone should have wasted words on it. After a while he said, "America. That's a fascinating country," as if he had never uttered a word against it. He talked about the trip to Genoa, about my lease, about my luggage. He went inside again and telephoned to Bindi, and came back to me. If we went by train he could have the car waiting for him when we got to Genoa. We might stop at Florence, since he had business to do there, and I had never seen it.

I wondered what Bindi was making of all this. To him, no doubt, it took its place at once among other, not outwardly dissimilar incidents. Viewing it from experience, he quite possibly foresaw the course and conclusion of it all; was already in possession of knowledge that we would only acquire in retrospect. Trapped in the events, we must live through them in order to learn the outcome.

When I began to gather the dishes together on the tray Gianni patted me and said, "There. You must admit old John does have a good idea once in a while."

"I love old John," I said, and laughed, and stuffed into my mouth the last piece of bread, which I had kept my eye on all this time.

# ❧ XIV ❧

As you go north from Naples on the train you pass for a mile or two through lines of poplars that have been netted together by screens of vines. The spaces between the trees are closed by broad, sagging spans of the vine-leaves, thick as a wall, interrupted only where the train passes among them as if through a series of parted curtains. The trees are so tall, the vines so dense, they look as if they have been cultivated for centuries. Going to Rome I had always watched for them after the stop at Pozzuoli; and, returning, they were the true outskirts of Naples. Now I pointed them out to Gianni as we sat opposite one another in a new fast train. The poplars were losing lemon-coloured leaves that drifted about them in the wind of that grey day, and the fabric of vines admitted light like a worn cloth.

"I forgot they would be bare."

"They're almost lovelier this way. A web, an anatomy. You can see how it all works."

I didn't like it so much though — the garlands slipping from the trees and the cord-like branches of the vines exposed — and regretted the fantastic barriers of green.

"This train," said Gianni as we swished and swayed. "It's acting so efficient that I'm afraid it's going to break down." But the train was supposed to take us to Florence in record time, and ultimately did so. Gianni was to see a colleague at Florence; and we were to stay there overnight and go on to Genoa by rail. I had let myself be consigned and re-consigned, agreeing to all his proposals, relieved to have proposals made. As Gioconda had said of him, "He thought of everything." It was even Gianni's idea that Serafina should take on the Colonel — who was remaining at Naples to hold, inevitably, the fort.

On our last evening in Naples, Gianni, who had come from Rome to fetch me, had found me sticking labels on my luggage, and he took one from me and pretended to paste it across my forehead.

"That's exactly how I feel," I said.

"I wouldn't be doing all this if it weren't for you," I told him now, in the train. He looked anxious. "I mean, you've done everything. You've thought of everything."

"Oh — women are hopeless at arranging journeys." I thought of Gioconda missing the plane at Malta, and knew he was thinking of it too. *"Paresse mentale,"* he said.

At first, in the train, he kept talking to diminish the sense of departure. When we had gone some miles, had passed the fields of poplars, he sat back looking pleased with himself and with me, in the way that a doctor attending to a wound will keep you diverted until the moment when he can surprise you by saying, "There now, it's all over," and show you the sealed or bound cicatrice, or the thorn he has extracted. So did Gianni try to distract my attention from the city that was now to have part of my attention always.

Grief would not quicken in me: I was indolent, replete. There was too much to take in, too many items to accommodate from a future that already suggested itself and impinged on the present. From too few clues I had to imagine another setting. The city of Washington was an enigma when seen on a map. It had been far easier to picture oneself, even if inaccurately, in Naples before leaving England: H Street is more difficult to conjure up in fancy than San Biagio dei Librai.

I said, "I remembered that I do know someone in Washington. There's a cousin of my sister-in-law's stationed there — a minor diplomat."

Gianni said, "All diplomats are minor."

I took up a newspaper that Gianni had bought at the station. There was a broad headline: Russia had put a dog into space. "Good lord," I said to Gianni. "Have you seen the news?"

"Yes," he said. "I meant to tell you. Bergman is divorcing Rossellini at last."

I watched the strip of the south being drawn past our

window, but its atmosphere was elusive now, so pressing was the intrusion of future into all my thoughts — the new world with its resourcefulness, its rectangles, its sexless news from outer space. I pictured the map of North America and sought to make a country of it, hewing out state after state. The train rushed along the foot of a stony hill, and on its other side we glimpsed ruins, a castle, white walls, and the sea.

I stood up to look. "A moulder'd citadel on the coast. An olive-hoary cape in ocean."

"What's that?"

"It's Tennyson." I thought, It will be something to get my language back.

"You'll miss poetry. There's not much of that in America." Gianni stroked my arm, looking up at me, then out of the window. "It won't be like this, over there."

"I have so many reasons to go there."

He nodded. "There are also the reasons you don't yet know about."

At Rome, the only stop, a middle-aged woman got into our compartment. She was short, sturdy, a spinster, and dying to talk. Leaning forward, she alertly held herself in readiness to participate in whatever conversation Gianni and I might have between ourselves, her bright eyes darting from one of us to the other in the hope of a break in our silence — for, after initial civilities, we were quiet. When we flashed through a station she would tell us encouragingly, "Orte" or "Orvieto," and I would smile and thank her and feel more than ever disinclined to talk. Somewhere near Chiusi her disappointment in us became conclusive, and she left us for another compartment — Gianni lifting down her suitcase from the rack and both of us, so to speak, wishing her better luck with our smiles and our farewells.

Gianni put his feet up again on the seat opposite, alongside the folds of my dress. "That woman was like a tinder box. One careless spark and we'd have had a conflagration."

I said, "We've been so private together. We're not used to being out and about." Everything between Gianni and me, until that morning, had taken place within my few rooms. Even the limitless prospect from those rooms opening on to the life of the bay had nurtured our apartness, as if we had been in a box at the opera.

I said this to Gianni, who agreed. "Italy's all a bit like that — one is always looking at something, surveying the scene, you know. The fact is, it's one of the last places left with a scene to be surveyed."

We were silent again until, confirming what he had just said, he raised a hand to the window. "Now if you look — no, there, right there, keep watching, that's it — you'll see the Duomo of Florence. We're about to arrive."

On a cold, brilliant November day, Gianni and I sat having lunch in the restaurant of our hotel at Florence.

Over his fettuccine Gianni ground the pepper mill as if he were wringing someone's neck. He had been doing business that morning at a villa out near San Casciano, and had come back full of fight. All the same, during those days the fight emptied out of him quickly: it was as if he allowed it an occasional token appearance to prove it hadn't been sham before, or to show that he hadn't faithlessly turned his back on all that. After a while he talked to me quite sensibly about his morning's work, dramatising nothing, and about the villa he had seen, with its great view of the Val di Pesa. His predicament had compelled him to some point of perspective, after all, and in a wild way I felt I had been good for him.

Gianni leant his elbow on the table and smoked. "It was in this room that I first saw my wife. Sitting over there, against that wall."

I looked across to where a blonde girl sat with a crewcut boy on a banquette. It was the first time Gianni had spoken of his wife.

"I couldn't take my eyes off her. She was with two men — her brother and a friend. She said later she had noticed me too — but I think that was just to be polite."

How tortuous, these strands of love — winding about us, entangling, strangling, wiggling their way across the crimson carpet of a restaurant, climbing the very walls.

Because his marriage was indissoluble, I had got into the habit of imagining Gianni as being always married,

married forever, and had never thought of a time when he and Gioconda were unattached; free, conceivably, had they met, to have married.

"Gianni, what are they like, your children?"

"Beautiful." It was the only completely secure utterance I ever heard from Gianni. It put him apart from the rest of us — Gioconda, Justin, me. It put us, quite irrationally, to shame.

I said to him, "I don't know why your having children should put us to shame, but it does. Why should it make such a difference? It's nothing, after all, having a child — there's no virtue in it, sometimes quite the contrary. Anyone can do it."

Gianni nodded. "In my case," he observed, "I may truly say as the English do, that it was as easy as falling on to a log."

Here was another piece of country Gioconda had traversed — these alien configurations of Gianni's existence which had given her pain, to which she had all but reconciled herself.

Our thoughts were the same, for after a while Gianni remarked to me, "You know that I once met Gioconda's father" — saying "you know" in the tone of one who is perfectly aware that you know nothing of the sort. "Rome," he went on, "the autumn of '45. Piazza Campitelli. I ran into some friends, they were on their way to a restaurant and asked me to come along. They were dining with this man . . . I very nearly refused, history professors weren't in my line. In fact history itself was none too popular with me at that moment. But he was quite a figure then — because of the war, you see — and I was at a loose end. So I went."

Gioconda's father had taken on such legendary quality for me that it was reassuring to find someone had actually set eyes on him.

"Well I have to admit," said Gianni, acknowledging with those words his true rival, "that he was pretty impressive. A great head of white hair, a brown face all seamed by worrying about the right things. A splendid use of language, something one finds in certain Neapolitans, single words forming entire narrations, phrases deployed like colour in a painting . . ." Gianni paused. "There was one thing, though." He waited for me to ask, then continued. "He had a set — it sounds unimportant — a whole set of medicines, little glass cylinders that he laid in a row by his plate, cutting them open one by one with a metal file he carried on him for the purpose. He made a ceremony of them, one felt one was being required to watch, it was an imposition. As I say, he was really rather terrific. I liked what he said, and the way he handled himself. But I couldn't help thinking — someone who does that in public, all those bottles — there must be something wrong."

"Gioconda knows that you met him?"

"It was how I first got in touch with her. I'd been told she didn't answer letters, no telephone, all that. So I wrote to her saying I had known her father — I stretched it a bit, for it was only that once that we'd met. When she replied I went to see her, and I told her how it was. Naturally," added Gianni, lowering his voice, "I didn't say all that about the medicines." He paused again, struck by the novelty of his having spared Gioconda anything. "By then he had got ill, had died, so the medicines were indicative in another way, sacrosanct."

"She never mentioned it to me — that you'd met him."

Gianni made a face. "It was one of those things — you know — that bothered her. Of course it does seem odd in retrospect, but she made too much of it, wondering this, wondering that, until I made her drop it. It's the South," said Gianni, as if Gioconda were no more to us than an example of regional idiosyncrasy. "They go in for that sort of thing.

"Jenny my dear," he said, touching my hand on the tablecloth. "It is all so long ago." But by this he meant to signify not the distance of these events, but the bond they had created.

The hotel concierge was getting us tickets for an early train to Genoa the following morning. One lunched on the train, which would reach Genoa that afternoon, and my ship sailed the same evening. It worried me, cutting things so fine.

"What if something went wrong?"

"What could possibly go wrong?" Gianni looked at

me wonderingly, as if nothing in his experience had ever given him cause to doubt the orderly progression of events, or the accomplishing of any projected undertaking.

We were in the train again, Gianni and I, waiting to leave Florence. This time it was I who had my feet up, and in Gianni's lap, as he tried to warm them between his palms. The train had stood in the station yard all night, the coldest night of that year. The heating operated in conjunction with the engine, which had not yet started up. We huddled in our corners, I with my gloved hands thrust in my sleeves and my icy shoes discarded; Gianni with his blue scarf rising around his ears. From time to time one of us would lower a hand to the gelid radiator vents below the seats, hoping to intercept a first tremor of warmth. Gianni was silent, his eyes on the platform, his hands slowly kneading my frozen toes.

Eventually he took off his scarf and wrapped it round my feet. I shook my head at him, and with a grimace he reassured me — it was as though we feared that speaking might make us colder. The gesture with which he drew the scarf from his throat brought Gioconda again to my mind, and a day when I had come into the courtyard at San Biagio and found her kneeling over her cat, which lay stunned there having jumped from an upper window after a moth. Gioconda, as I watched, pulled off her cardigan to cover the animal, making a soft place for its

head with a folded sleeve. This pelican-like instinct —
for the cat had no need of covering that warm day — to
tear something from oneself in order to palliate the
emergency of another creature is so strong as to be a
primitive manifestation, rather than a refinement, of
human sympathy. Perhaps that is why Saint Martin only
offered half of his cloak to the beggar.

On the otherwise empty platform a group of adolescent boys were playing the fool, knocking each other
about to keep warm; and Gianni, watching them, remarked sadly, "When Italians are silly, they are sillier
than anybody."

Gianni and I were private once again, separated from
the scene for the last time. We might have been the only
passengers on that cold train — which stirred at length
and with metallic groans breathed its stuffy heat into us
and over the thick upholstery, and slowly jolted from the
station towards its first resting place at Pisa. We trundled
through suburbs of Florence, and on to a plain of fields
so bleakly divested of summer that they gave the impression of having been cleared of wreckage.

A guard came and took our tickets, a boy brought us
hot coffee and promised us lunch later on. An older man
in a white jacket put his head round the door and asked
if we had any requests to make.

"It's like being in the condemned cell," Gianni remarked. "They'll be sending the priest in next." He released my feet and let me put my shoes on. He leant

across and kissed me. "Do you remember," he said, "when I kissed you at Herculaneum, that first time?"

"That was hateful." It was curious that he should seem more faithful to Gioconda now than he had then.

"You looked at me as if I'd uttered some intolerable banality."

"Yes. I was furious the whole afternoon." We were like a couple discovering the origins, tracing the course of their love.

"I don't know how this will seem to you —" meaning our time together, Gianni indicated the compartment with a splaying of his fingers — "looking back."

"Much as it does now, I expect."

"I don't even know how it seems to you now."

"Like a great courtesy. An act of rescue."

"The rescue is all the other way," he said, but after a while added, "It is my specialty, the act of rescue."

Another time he said to me, "Are you sure, won't you blame me for this, for all of this? Because a woman like you, you would only — would rather — do this for love."

"You might say, I have done it for love." For their love, I meant: his and Gioconda's.

"No, that's rubbish. It's too far-fetched. And not even desirable. I am not so lofty in my thinking, I assure you — though in this case not entirely despicable either. I meant, will it seem, afterwards, like another renunciation?"

"It ought to, no doubt. Instead it feels more like choosing."

"Not just a label I pasted on you? Here." He laid his hand to my forehead as if testing me for fever.

"That was for the journey. I chose the destination."

"One where I cannot come."

We both knew it to be otherwise, to be worse than that: for he could come, but would not.

All that morning we moved up the coast of Italy, past hills and promontories, uplands crowned with chapels and castles, slopes of orchards and vineyards. Stone farms and rose-walled villas ascended terraces of autumn fields, or stood forward from autumnal woods. The sea, when it appeared on our other hand, was level, brilliant, bordered with a motionless litter of summer towns and shuttered bathing places.

"What I like about the landscape of Italy," Gianni informed me, "is that there's none of this nonsense about the great outdoors. That sort of thing's all right elsewhere. Here you could practically say it's an indoor landscape. It's Nature with beautiful manners — no, that's too tame. Rather, it's as if Nature were capable of thought, of joy."

Neither of us mentioned the volcano.

Above our lunch tray we sighted the Apuan mountains. "Gianni, look. There's already snow up there."

"That's not snow. Those are the scars of the quarries. Soon we'll be passing the towns where they bring the marble down — Pietra Santa, Forte dei Marmi. Up there, though, it's fascinating — those men in the quarries have an existence that has nothing to do with ours. It's as if they're at work on the mountains of the moon." It turned out that Gianni had made a documentary once, some fanciful factual version of Michelangelo's life in the quarries at Carrara. "He built a road there, Michelangelo. We recreated the conditions, as they say: what presumption — if only we could. We had the men banging away at any old boulder — just for the picture, you know — had them shivering or sweating to denote the seasons. They thought we were lunatics, those men at the quarries . . . I learnt a lot up there. The mountains take revenge on the men — kill them in all sorts of ways, with falls, accidents, through the lungs; places are like that, like people, they don't care to be exploited and they find ways of avenging themselves. When the masons try to remove the marble in monoliths, it thwarts them by cracking; when they want it in sections, it splits in just the wrong place. The men talk about the stone as if it's active. As if it had a will and destiny of its own. Beautiful, the marble — round here it's mostly white, further north it's green, rose around Verona."

It was Gianni's best show of patriotism, this pleasure in the coloured stones of his country.

At Sestri Levante the guard came by for the last time.

"What was that about the frontier?" I asked Gianni when we were alone again.

"He wanted to be sure we were getting out at Genoa. There's one carriage that goes on, you see — this one. Goes beyond Ventimiglia. Crosses into France."

"Into France — to where?"

"Oh . . . Monte Carlo, I suppose. Nice. Cannes."

It made Gioconda seem very near, this same train going on to Nice, these same reticulated luggage racks and seats of bristly plush fetching up practically on her doorstep this very night. I thought how Gianni must have imagined staying on the train, reaching her this evening. If it were not for me, how soon he might be there.

"Rapallo," Gianni said. "We'll soon be there."

Approaching Genoa, leaving Italy, drawn along between these hills (that were now contoured with social prestige, posted with the villas of the rich: hills of a portentous topographical melancholy unknown at Naples, as if the landscape itself were missing its own past) and the sea, it was not apprehension that increased in me, but the sense of place. If places were vengeful, as Gianni said, they were also more magnanimous than any human benefactor, making provision for us for the rest of our lives, asking nothing more of us than to take pleasure in their memory. Gioconda had said it was a way to go on caring about a place, to miss it; yet it was rather, for me, that there now existed at last a place that could be missed. Arriving in America, I was coming from this. Some part of me would always be coming, now, from this. Like the dye they had injected into my veins, the country coloured my essence, illuminated the reaction to everything else. Here, literally, I had come to my senses.

Unimaginable to my relatives, even had they been informed of them, were the circumstances of my sitting there in the train, every fact and object unrelated to their concept of my past. The inconceivability of ever explaining was the measure of distance from them now. They were like people who have been interrupted in the telling of some story and who, even were they to resume, could never manage now to make their point: the impetus, the timing, the advantage had been lost.

Thinking about this new past of mine — that was still the present, though imagination leapt ahead to seal it from the perspective of departure — I contrasted it with what had hitherto served me for a past: that other past, of exile, of Africa and England, Edmund and Norah. And it was as if I had come upon old letters addressed in a hand unrecollected but poignantly familiar, an envelope over which the hand may tremble but which must be opened before the writer can be identified. So must I eventually retrace these sources of self — later on, as the search drew closer to home. Aspects of remorse, of injury, of forgetfulness would make their belated bridges over courses that had run dry, or been diverted. Justin had been the last of it, a transition.

Here, at the moment of arrival, the point of departure, Justin in this way re-entered my experience and made himself wondered about.

"It isn't so far from here," said Gianni. "The frontier. A couple of hours from Genoa, that's all."

And so, each thinking of another, we arrived.

Gianni and I were walking on the deck of a ship. Children ran past us, there were women in fur coats, a young man with red roses, a steward with a basket of fruit enclosed in cellophane. The ship itself, similarly enclosed in warm air, smelt of food, paint, deodoriser, anything but the sea. Indoors there were sofas and armchairs, and an enormous bar. It was as if a piece of land were casting off, instead of a vessel.

"Gianni, you could have gone on to France this evening."

He shook his head. "Just as soon pass the night here. No sense killing oneself for the sake of a few hours."

There was, in his manner of saying this, something endearingly, uncharacteristically gauche — so unpractised was Gianni in the art of dissembling his own good actions — that touched me as much as his delicacy in not going instantly, as he must have wished to do, from me to Gioconda, but allowing, instead, a single night to intervene. It was an act of almost formal observance: the sort of tribute you might pay to the dead.

I pressed his arm as we walked. "After this, anything's possible."

"Anything was possible *before* this, too; but you didn't know it."

I could picture, in the space of a second or two, his early start tomorrow on the twisting drive, the mountains descending clear to the sea, the road signs changing to French; his sense of solitude in the car all tapering away from me, all shaped to the imminence of meeting Gioconda. And his arrival. It was so much of a piece with what I had known of them that I could scarcely credit I was to have no part in it — as I stood on the deck, cut off already from their joy, imagining how they would walk perhaps tomorrow along the seafront with their arms about each other. So utterly did this future belong only to them that I could not even ask of Gianni whether he would tell our story, his and mine.

Every few minutes a voice went off like an alarm clock, shaking at us. *"La nave è in partenza,"* and then in English, "The sheep is living." Stirred by the wash of a tug, the deck swung softly, suggesting its power like an animal in captivity.

"You have to go," I told him.

We leant on the rail. There were some inches of dirty water, then the soiled timbers of a pier. A couple beside us discreetly turned away, seeing us in tears.

"They think we're lovers," Gianni said. "They think it's something simple like that."

"Gianni," I said. "My darling, please go."

He said to me, "This is awful," as if he had expected something else. "Is there nothing but this?"

"Please go. Go quickly."

He took my face between his hands and kissed me on either cheek — as if I were a member of his family, or a hero. "Dear, lovely Jenny. Be brave. Be happy. Never forget." I felt the separate pressure of his fingers, the texture of his skin and clothes. And then the vacancy where these had been.

Leaning again on the rail, I saw him, below, emerge from the covered gangway and set off along the pier. Although the dark was coming down, he had put on sunglasses to hide his tears and, because of this, people stared after him — thinking, perhaps, that he was some public figure, an artist, possibly, or an actor, who on this occasion wished to be his private self and depart unrecognised.

# ❧ XV ❧

So much was being carried along, carried away: the carved frame of a chair, uncushioned; a glassless mirror in which the bearer's head showed, unreflected; the empty metal outline of a garden table, tilted between two staggering men; cups of coffee borne on chromium discs by boys in stained white coats. It was like an exodus, everyone had something of the city in his hands.

Outside the building an old man was carrying the shaft of a Doric column on his shoulder. When I got out of the taxi I saw it was a roll of pale, corrugated plastic, the sort that is used to roof a terrace or make a sloping shelter for a car.

A fat girl in curlers put her head out of the *portiere*'s window. "Was she —" she reached back to subdue her transistor — "was she expecting you?"

"I wrote from Rome at the beginning of the week. The telephone doesn't answer."

Rome impressed her. "From Rome, imagine. Well — she's been away, in and out. That's the way it is, this time of year."

"Shall I go up?"

"You can try. Perhaps there's someone."

She watched me go on, into the courtyard. Because I hesitated she thought I had lost the way. "To the left," she shouted. And *"Coraggio."* A man came out of the driving school to see what was going on, and stayed to see what would come next.

The stairs had been lighted — there was a begrimed switch at the foot of them, and a twisted cord was tacked in loops along the wall. But the light did not work. So that after all it was like before and one went up in darkness.

A voice came down, tender, desperate. "Let me dream that you love me again —"

No need to ring, for both doors were open and a woman I had never seen was polishing the handles and lock, and the brass knocker. She was squat and low-browed, and wore an overall of dark flowers.

"And let me die in my dream," she sang, the word dream fading as she applied the duster, with her finger-tip, to the brass doorbell, causing it to wobble through a few sporadic, strangled calls. Seeing me, she stood straight, the duster in one hand and a reeking tin of polish in the other. "Signora?"

I could see past her into the hallway where, on a mat of wrinkled brocade, my letter lay with others on a table; as Gioconda's own letter had lain, years ago.

"Do you expect her?" I asked, giving Gioconda

neither name nor designation. For she might have married; and it was strange to me to bring out her name again, at last.

The woman said, "She has gone to the island."

"Is Tosca here?"

"Dear lady," said this woman. "Tosca is dead, poor thing."

The way she talked. Everything was a pronouncement, as if she had never had to utter commonplaces.

"I haven't been here for a long time."

"Tosca died — well, it has been five years, six years. Poor thing."

Inside, a pale cat sauntered through variegated shadows in the hall. By the long heavy flanks and wide head I was misled into imagining that it could be Iocasta, and when it turned to stare at me with a mask half-extinguished by a long blotch of black, the revelation was absurdly horrifying.

"Will she come back?" It was not Tosca, now, we spoke of.

"In a few days." The woman spread her hands, the duster one way, the polish the other. "At this time of year —" it was the end of winter, the start of spring — "she is often away."

"How can I — where is she staying?"

She didn't know — and this too seemed to be an answer. The cat came out to the landing and looked at me with its frightening face. Knowing I did not want it,

humourlessly it passed itself from ear to tail along my
leg.

"If you go to the island, you'll find her in the piazza.
Sitting in the café."

I myself would never make such a statement without
in some way qualifying it. But she did not spoil her
oracular utterance — made it, in fact, the more com
pelling — when after a moment she repeated it. "You
will find her sitting in the café."

I gave her a couple of coins, more from admiration
than gratitude, and she was genuinely shocked by them.
"No. Absolutely not," she said, hiding them in the pocket
of her apron as if they were unsightly.

Because now I must go further than I thought, I did
not stop to give an account of my findings to the deputa
tion in the *cortile* — unsportingly; but it was in this way
that I learnt Gioconda was unmarried still. As I walked
out to the street, under the archway, a window was flung
up in the courtyard behind and the sybil's voice called
down to them, "It's a foreigner."

"Yes, from Rome."

"She's after the Signorina."

I had to take the last ferry, which happened to be the
*aliscafo* — one of those vessels, looking like a space
ship, that rip about the Mediterranean these days. In fact
the journey was altered in every detail, as if each move
of memory were being meticulously checkmated and
penalised. The *aliscafo* did not leave from the port as

all, but from the mole at Mergellina at the other end of the town; one did not have a coffee on board, waiting for the boat to cast off, but stood at the end of the pier in cold twilight until the machine came thudding and spinning alongside; and hurried aboard before she could blast off again. I had been relying on the slow transition of the boat trip, a couple of hours, to do the work of years, setting my thoughts like sails towards our meeting; now that I was to be hurtled across the harbour in a fraction of the time, it was possible to blame, on that surprise, all one's unreadiness.

Thoughts were as little to be commanded as events. It was Tosca who kept coming to mind as we waited, small group of passengers, at the tip of the mole. I remembered how Gioconda had told me, from her mother's account, of Tosca's arrival in their house — a country girl, barefoot, carrying her belongings swathed in a bundle on her head. Tosca, almost grim, almost wordless, part Northerner, would take time to know, I used to think; and now there was no time to know her, and all the time in the world. Had she disliked Gianni, had she disliked me? Had she a private life of crises and sorrows that ran, undivulged, parallel to ours?

It was as if, in going to Gioconda's house, I had turned up at the scene of an accident — that it might just as easily have been Gioconda's death that I had learnt of, and that her survival, rather than Tosca's, was a matter of pure chance.

The principle of our boat — to outstrip the elements

rather than adapt to them — made itself felt at once, outstripping thought and sensation, causing one to feel involuntarily propelled to the island, as if this weird vessel were the visible form of forces beyond our control. It mocked, with its frenzied velocity, the constancy of the two points within which we moved — the city rising astern of us, and ahead of us the island in darkness.

At first we followed the shelter of the Posillipo, too fast for any house to be distinguished, for now it was all houses, the cape itself was like a single house and the rest but windows in it. Everything familiar roared and spun by, drained of significance by our pace, our noise. Evidence boiled about meaninglessly, as in the moment before a swoon.

Of the few other passengers I could see only a businessman doing his crossword puzzle on a plunging table, a chic young couple in turtlenecks and trousers, and a tawny matron in leopard skin who pitilessly smoked at us, lifting up a wrist from which the charm bracelet shook as violently as if she were in shock. No homing Caprese would have taken this costly boat when there was the earlier, habitual boat, the *vaporetto*: this was the barque of Pucci, Gucci, and Ferragamo, no question.

Now everything was tinged with agitation. The vessel induced panic, one could only think of what might go wrong. It came to me that Gioconda might be shockingly aged, might be ill, fat, thin — might bear any unforeseeable mark of the intervening years. It occurred to me for instance, that she might have cut off her hair: this idea was dreadful — as though cropped hair had carried some implication, such as her having been a nun or a convict. It caused the same spasm of horror that had seized me at San Biagio over the streaked face of the cat. I tried out all these impressions on myself, seeking to exorcise them, to make them less likely by anticipating them. It was no use, and it was going to be unimaginable like everything else — like Tosca, like the *aliscafo*, like the immense chimney of a new skyscraper that, central as a maypole, made nonsense of the city's dimensions.

Overwhelmed in false perspective I wondered if she would remember me. Like an actor's loss of confidence, rupturing the filament of performance, was the question, Why have I come.

For it was impossible now to give this journey its intended, official seal of past revisited. All these passing moments moved towards some future whole, some time fulfilled: it would be long before they became part of any foreseeable past. "FLY TO TURKEY," said the Alitalia advertisement on the businessman's newspaper. Although I wished I hadn't come, it did not occur to me to go back. In matters of importance there is no such thing as "best avoided" — avoidance is only a vacuum that something else must fill. Everything is the inevitable.

(Five years after I sailed from Genoa, and some years before this ride on the *aliscafo*, a film appeared over Gianni's name, made from a screenplay by Gioconda. It was the story of a man who has managed to divert the course of his existence so often and so successfully that in middle age he is no more than a set of tributaries of indefinite origin and negligible momentum. As a child he evades, by fostering a minor illness, the boarding school that has maltreated his brother; as a youth, by buying himself into a protected occupation, he remains behind when his contemporaries depart to be slaughtered on the Russian front. The pattern becomes less rational, more obsessive — is repeated in a convenient marriage, in the repudiation of a pleasurable but unspectacular talent, in successive adaptations to popular causes. As the film ends, the man is building a house in a country which bores him but where he can live out his life without paying taxes.

This film was called, in English, *Cause for Congratulation*, and I saw it one afternoon at a theatre on Upper Broadway together with a Swedish film about schizophrenia. When it first appeared it was unfavourably compared with the earlier collaboration, *Del Tempo Felice*; but that equivocal reception was the prelude to its acquiring a particular reputation, being revived in art cinemas, and cited as an outstanding example — of some technique or other — by the same experts who initially disparaged it. I am told this is the natural sequence in such affairs, and that in fact it could not have happened otherwise.)

I wished Gioconda might have been forewarned. In

this my arrival was like our first meeting, unapprehended by her. That we were to meet in public — for I did not doubt that I would find her sitting in the café — must restrict our show of reunion, perhaps reduce us to an exchange of platitudes: "You are just the same" or "It seems like yesterday."

It does not seem like yesterday. Surviving such change, such accelerations of change, with continuity — if continuity still exists — moving beyond the speed of cognisance, it is more as if we had been reincarnated centuries later than had lived through such dispersals and invalidations, such desuetude. That epoch, our time at Naples, seems historic now. It doesn't seem like modern life. But it didn't seem like modern life then either, it was more like life than modern life, more lifelike, livelier, likelier: relics are not the less obsolete for their superior vitality — like the vineyard that has been left to flourish intact on the Vomero, among the deadly apartment buildings, not so much showing how it was as what has happened to it.

I remember how Gianni cautioned us about the great eruption and I wonder if we will go on talking and joking, eating and taking baths, until we are found petrified, with our stone hands before our faces warding off the inevitable.

The engine subsiding, we re-enter the elements. It is dark, the boat comes splashing quite tamely into port and the journey recedes, throbbing, like a toothache. There are lights, colours, large-eyed faces of pale people on the breakwater and the soundless up and down movements of their feet stamping with cold. The vessel submits to a few superficial ministrations — is tied up with rope like any other vessel and has a gangplank fastened to her side. The leopard bends her cigarette into a tin ashtray; she stands ahead of me in the line to disembark, her tawny head bound with a speckled scarf, tilted by the backward stance with which she clasps her square dressing-case — both hands clenched around its central handle as urgently as if she were getting into a lifeboat. We shuffle, we descend.

The outcome of such a crossing is immaterial. One can only discover what has already come into existence. Equipped to search, we justify ourselves by ranging as far afield as possible, in order to render a plausible account, to be able to say, "I looked everywhere." But it is not by such journeys as these that one approaches home. Rather, they are, like Gioconda's trip to Madison Avenue, a garland laid upon experience. At most, they serve to establish that the object of search is not this, is elsewhere; to eliminate natural but unfounded suppositions. We are like those early explorers of Australia who died of thirst on expeditions to the dead centre of a continent, always thinking they must come ultimately to water — to an inland sea, to a lake, a river, a cascade. Deceived by salt deposits, by rivers that flow inland, by the fossils of seashells, they were driven on by incredulity as well — by disbelief that one could come so far without drawing nearer to what one sought.

So with these other explorations. There is much digression, despite improved techniques. We take our bearings from the wrong landmark, wish that when young we had studied the stars; name the flowers for ourselves and the deserts after others. When the territory is charted, its eventual aspect may be quite other than what was hoped for. One can only say, it will be a whole — a region from which a few features, not necessarily those that seemed prominent at the start, will stand out in clear colours. Not to direct, but to solace us; not to fix our positions, but to show us how we came.

## ABOUT THE AUTHOR

SHIRLEY HAZZARD has written five other
books: four works of fiction (*Cliffs of Fall, People
in Glass Houses, The Evening of the Holiday,* and
*The Transit of Venus*); and *Defeat of an Ideal,* a
study of the United Nations, where she worked for
some years. Many of her short stories have been
published in *The New Yorker;* her work has re-
ceived, among other recognition, a First Prize in
the O. Henry Short Story awards. She is the
winner of the 1981 National Book Critics Circle
Award for *The Transit of Venus*.

Shirley Hazzard was born in Australia. She
now lives in New York with her husband, Francis
Steegmuller.

# PLAYBOY NOVELS OF HORROR AND THE OCCULT

# ABSOLUTELY CHILLING